GHETTO GIRLS 3

ANTHONY WHYTE

AUGUSTUS
PUBLISHING

Copyright 2006 by Anthony Whyte
ISBN: 0975945351

Edited by Tracy Sherrod
Design/Photogaphy: Jason Claiborne
GraphPainting: Kel1st.com

First printing Augustus Publishing paperback November 2006

AUGUSTUS
PUBLISHING

AugustusPublishing.com
33 Indian Road New York, New York 10034

ACKNOWLEDGEMENTS

Through God all is possible.

Thanks to Tracy Sherrod for the edits and cuts.

Jay Clay & the Augustus Publishing manuscript team,

Tamiko Maldonado, Star and the poet, Joy Leftow

Yasmin Sangaria and Janet for the photo shoot.

Kel1st and Annabelle for your tireless work

Good-looking all friends and physicals down with me

To all the readers for supporting

Thank you all

One love,

Anthony Whyte

PROLOGUE

Deedee, Eric, Coco and Josephine arrived at the studio. This opportunity to record in the studio with famed producer Eric Ascot was her prize for winning the talent show sponsored by Busta. First prize included not only money but also a chance to do a single and possibly an album.

"Coco this might be your one shot," Josephine said. "This might be the moment your career is launched and I'll be glad to say I was there."

"Chill out, you're making me nervous, yo," Coco said.

"What's good? You finished with the tracks?" Eric asked rap producers, Silky Black and Show Biz.

"Everything is set. You can take it from right where the beat drops," Show Biz said and gave Eric a pound.

"The track is kind a hot. I laid some new sounds on it. Lemme hear it when you mix it down and add the other vocals, ahight E?" Silky Black requested.

"Coco we throw sump'n, sump'n up there for you. Show

Biz said turning to the girls. We need about thirty-two bars from you to set it off. Eric will show you what I'm talking 'bout."

The girls walked into the studio. Eric Ascot directed them to the lounge area filled with television sets and vending machines. A pool table was bare and unused.

"Coco I got this track that I want to use for a Silky Black song. It was just going to be his vocals but I wanted to try a thing and get a verse or two from you on it."

"This is something I've been looking forward to doing," Coco answered enthusiastically.

"Josephine will also do some background stuff, so we'll get everyone involved." Eric continued.

"Wait a minute Uncle E. I don't hear my name being called?" Deedee frowned. Eric walked over and put his hand around her shoulder, "I've got something very special planned for you. Only you can handle this task. I'll discuss it later."

"Okay, it better be something important," Deedee said.

"Alright, let's go invade the studio," Eric said leading the way.

Eric Ascot and Coco sat facing each other at the sound-board.

The engineer slipped a disk into the drive and musical notes danced across the computer screen. The earth shook as the sound was filtered through Klipschs 911 studio size speakers. Coco was transported to a musical wonderland. The speakers vibrated and a steady sound of Hip-Hop came through heavy and inflexible. Coco jerked from her torso to the top of her head. She was feeling the whole thing.

"It's yours, when you're ready, just go in the booth," Eric announced.

He disappeared as the bass led the horns that ushered the percussion.

She worked the mechanics of the beat, breaking it down, and then spat freestyle lyrics that hit like an automatic weapon.

Niggers terrified when they hear what comes from the young one...

Coco's in your town put down your guns have fun...

This lyrical gift is like Teflon can't say I won't kill anyone...

I ain't just rapping to be popular step to me I'll bury ya...

The Teflon things come flyin atcha...

In the race for cheddar I'm natural born killa...

Hustla running laps like I'm a track star...

Oh yeah hip-hop-hooray in case you forgot I say...

Coco's getting ghetto n your town today...

A champion like Laila my rhymes lay you out forever...

Try to peep me but can't see my phantom jab coming to smash ya ...

You cold before you feel me suckas?"

There was a loud howl and scattered applause, some

present in the studio laughed. Coco's verse off the top of her dome served to convince all that she was ready for the next level.

ONE

No Standing Any Time

Read the sign above the black, Range Rover on chromes. The rims were still spinning and two burly body-guards remained seated in plush leather, air condition comfort, waiting for Deedee's return. One of them doubled as a chauf-feur, sat in the driver's seat. The other, remote in hand, switched the radio dial to a local station.

The news and weather report were in progress: "March 9 97 Biggie Smalls was shot to death out in LA while listening to his joint; *I'm going back to Cali...* Today on the sixth anniver-sary of his death we will remember the legend coming right after the weather. Right now New York stand up... Fordham Road in the Bronx, Jamaica Ave, Queens... up in the streets of Harlem... you're in tune to the best Hip Hop 'n' R&B sounds in town. It's three 'o' five and right about now we'd like to take it back to the streets of Brooklyn with the sounds of Notorious B.I.G. This is 'Warning.'"

The disk jockey said his piece and a raw, pulsating drum and bass laced with the lyrical flow of rap legend, Biggie Smalls followed. The classic knocked hard through the streets.

> *...Who the hell is this?*
>
> *Paging me at 5:46 in the morning*
>
> *Crack a dawn now I'm yawn n,*
>
> *wipe the cold out my eye,*
>
> *See who's this paging me and why...?*

The rhythmic spit of the Notorious B.I.G. banged clear through Bose Acoustics Systems speakers echoing through the hectic, city sidewalk, reverberating from buildings. The sound almost over shadowed the sight of several people running from out of the same building Deedee and her friend went into earlier.

"What d'ya thinks is going down?" The curious bodyguard asked.

"Where?" The driver answered with a shrug. Without taking a second glance, he went back to bopping his head to the rap legend.

> *...It's my nigga pop from the barbershop*
>
> *Told me he was in the gambling spot*
>
> *and heard the intricate plot...*

"Sump'n gotta be up..." The grumble came from the concerned bodyguard.

The driver peered from smoked window and mumbled something inaudible. He saw the clamor in front of the building but quickly dismissed it.

"Nah, sump'n definitely up," the guard said.

"I'm saying ya always see niggas running," the driver quipped. "Most o' them don't even know why they running. They just run to be running. Like my man, Cedric the Entertainer sez, 'don't take much to set black folks off running.' Niggas think they hear sump'n strange they ain't turning around to find out what happened? They be like 'see ya.'" The driver chuckled. A few more people darted from the building as if it was on fire.

"Sump'n ain't right. Deedee went up in that building, and as far as I know, she's still up there. We getting paid to make sure nothing goes wrong with her. Matter fact, it was her Uncle who said 'Make sure no harm comes to not even a strand of her hair.' I'm a go take a look, ahight." He checked his weapon and exited the vehicle.

"I ain't mad. I'll be right here. Hit me if there's problems." The driver held his cell phone high.

The bodyguard walked away from the vehicle and headed to the entrance of the building.

"What's going on up in there?" He asked pointing to the building where a couple of teens were pitching.

"A bunch a bitches up on the third floor arguing 'bout some man or sump'n, you know the usual. But big man, big man check this out we got dat, ya heard?" Before he could turn toward the door, he overheard a conversation. "Man, you know that bitch straight up lesbian, man. That bitch ain't fighting over no man that bitch fighting over some other bitch."

"Ah, there you go again hatin' cuz the bitch ain't givin' *you* none, petty ass nigga."

"I ain't bout it like that, cuz I got mines."

"Man, leave me alone. I got what you need right here."

The burly bodyguard walked away leaving the two teens still pitching.

"Fighting?" He repeated perplexed, then gathered speed only to bump into another teen on his way out the building. Walking fast and breathing hard the bodyguard attempted to engage him.

"Hey yo, hey yo, yeah you, what's going on up in the building?"

The teen paused shrugged her shoulders before saying: "I don't know man," she said out of breath.

"These girls were scrapping on the third floor and one o' them pulled out a hammer and let off," another person volunteered as she quickly moved past the bodyguard.

When the beefy security reached the third floor, he heard a chilling scream over his heavy breathing.

"Someone please call 911!" Coco cried for help. The guard hurriedly sought Deedee and grabbed her by the arm.

"Are you okay?" He asked with urgency.

"Yes, yes I'm fine," Deedee said as her fingers frantically worked her cell phone. "We have an emergency. What's the name of these houses?" Deedee asked repositioning herself trying to get better transmission.

"Ah... Malcolm X," someone shouted.

"Ah... I'm not sure. I can't hear you... I don't have good reception. An older lady might be dead..."

Coco grabbed the phone, "We need an ambulance right

away, someone fired a gun and a lady is down... I don't know? Just send the ambulance right away thank you. It's the corner of one-tenth and Lenox, hurry." Coco hurried back to where Miss Katie's body laid. "The ambulance will be here soon, Miss Katie. Please hold on it won't be long now. Please hold on." Coco held her hand pleading, tears streaming.

"Coco, maybe we should move her inside, I'll ask the bodyguard to help carry her..."

"You think she's dead, Dee?"

"I don't know Coco. She's not moving. Is she breathing or anything...?"

"I can hardly tell. Miss Katie, Miss Katie, Miss Katie..." Coco cowered as she wailed over Miss Katie's body. "Damn, why?"

Deedee tried to hug Coco but the bodyguard came and pulled her away.

"We gotta go. The ambulance is on its way. I think she can handle it from here," he said.

"Let me go." Deedee ordered. "I have to stick around. Coco is going to need me. After these two ah...bimbos on the elevator jumped us and when the police come I'll have to..."

"It's all good, Dee. It wasn't your beef to begin with. Kim and I have been going at it for a minute now."

"What about the other girl with her? She shot at us."

"Dee, I appreciate it and all, but you don't have to get involved any further. I told you, this bullshit been going on between them two and me, ever since that nigga, Deja's been murk."

"Deja?"

"Call me I'll tell you later." The girls hugged and Coco sat next to Miss Katie's body.

On the street, Deedee stepped into the parked Range Rover and watched as the police led the way into the building with firefighters and the EMTs in the rear.

TWO

Coco winced from the pain that she felt in her chest. The slow moving emergency teams, toying around with their equipment, appearing unsure, was too annoying.

"Please yo, yo please what're y'all doing bout her yo?" Coco asked feeling a sharp pain searing her stomach. She folded her arms and watched the police fan out, sniffing for a lead. The paramedics looked dumbfounded.

"For real for real, y'all gotta start doing' sump'n, Miss Katie could die, yo. C'mon, already, yo," Coco said, watching the paramedics stare at each other then at her. "What da fuck, am I the only one around here who understands English? There's an old lady laid out on the floor and y'all need to get busy and do sump'n. Do y'all jobs and stop looking at the hood rats!"

"Young lady, please get back in your apartment and watch yourself, you don't want to see the inside of a cell tonight," an approaching officer said.

"I don't care. Tell humpty and his corny ass pal, dumpy in those damn paramedics uniforms to start acting like they came here to save lives not grab ass. All they be doing since they got up in here is staring at every bitches' ass, when they should be doing sump'n to save this lady."

"Okay, okay, but please calm yourself. Turn it down a notch. We must make sure the area is safe. The medics must feel secure before anything else happens. Now you wouldn't want either of these medics to be ah, shot while doing their job, saving a life, right?" The officer sarcastically asked while menacingly spinning his nightstick.

Coco made a face, sulked and turned away. The officer nodded to the paramedics and they went to work on Miss Katie.

"Possible heart attack," the paramedic yelled into a hand held radio. "Victim is African American, approximate age sixty-five. There does not appear to be any visible gunshot wounds."

Coco could feel the tightness increasing in her chest as she realized that there would be no one else to share her deepest feelings. She was caught up in the memories of Miss Katie as the officer tried to get her attention.

"Who had guns?"

"Was she shot?"

"Were you a witness?"

"What was she doing alone in the hallway?"

"Was this a stick-up?"

Coco remained tightlipped despite hearing the questions. She cringed as she witnessed the EMTs' attempts to revive Miss Katie. Their actions were almost brutal. One minute they were shifting the body this way, then another way. Tears continued to roll down Coco's cheeks while she listened to the paramedics shout above the curious crowd.

"Coming through! Coming through!"

"Make way! Give us some room people!" The paramedics were rolling Miss Katie's immobilized frame on a two-man stretcher. Coco closed the door to Miss Katie's place and followed the paramedics to the elevator just as the door closed. She raced down the stairs.

In the lobby, she slid by police officers interviewing neighbors about the shooting incident. She ran after the paramedics but the uniformed officers would not let her get close to the ambulance.

"Are you a relative?" One of the medical technicians asked while placing a breathing apparatus over Miss Katie's nose and mouth.

"I... I'm her relative. She's like... ah she's ah my grandmother..."

"Do you know if she's got medical coverage?"

"I guess... ah... I mean I could check."

"What do you know?"

"Look, just give me a list of whatever you need and I'll get it for you. Please get her to a hospital!"

"Alright, alright, cool it, we're only here to help, not to have a fight," the technician said, then wrote on a sheet and gave it to Coco. "Here, call this number and the operator will let you know the hospital where she'll be admitted. Bring everything on the list to that hospital."

"Done," Coco said and took the note. "Take care of her, please."

"Back up, please."

The technician slammed the door. Coco stood with her arms folded, watching and praying until the ambulance disappeared from her view. Coco felt her strength sapped, as if the whole building had just collapsed on her. Her heart tightened with fear as her tears came in a rush. She ingored the call of an officer. Coco lit a cigarette and sucked deeply on it. She exhaled and contemplated her escape from this crowd.

"We have to speak with you," the officer said.

"I really have nothing to say to y'all. I've got to go and help the old lady that was hurt," Coco hastily answered.

"I understand you Miss, but I've got to get a statement regarding what caused it all. Some of your neighbors reported that you know who fired the gun," the officer countered.

"All right, all right, there were a couple of girls fighting or sump'n and then one of them pulled out a gun and bust it. I ducked like everyone else and got da hell outta dodge. Therefore, I couldn't see anything. You feel me, officer?"

"Do you know the name of the girl who had the gun and fired the shot?"

"Nah, nah I don't know those peeps. I don't know any of them. I heard people saying that they were visiting. They ain't from this building. That's all I know. That's it, yo."

"One more thing, what's your name? And how can I get a hold of you? "

"Why?"

"Just in case we've..."

"Y'all don't need my info then next thing I know, peeps gonna be thinking I'm down with Five-Oh. I ain't down," Coco said straining her neck. She thumped her cigarette then turned and ran upstairs. She left the officer staring in opened-mouth disbelief.

THREE

Lil' Long sneaked out of the recreation room with Ernesto. He had known Ernesto somewhat, from back on the streets. Now locked up in the same facility everything was tight between them. Both slid into an office next to the recreation room. It was a counselor's office.

Soon two fat female correction officers joined them. The officers frisked them including a thorough body search. To make sure all cavities were appropriately checked, the COs' dropped to their knees. Then Lil' Long and Ernesto sat down, leaned back as they received head courtesy of the females. Both Lil' Long and Ernesto lit cigars.

"Yeah man I gotta get outta this place, dogs," Lil' Long said.

"Ah... mami, yeah ah... hmm... take it easy, mami. Be easy with Nesto's dong," Ernesto said enjoying the carnal pleasures of the correction officer's lips, while listening to Lil' Long.

"You listening to me dogs? I can't wait to get da fuck

up."

"Ah, hmm. You don't like the way it's being run here or sump'n, daddy?"

"Man it's all good, but ain't nuthin like being out in da muthafuckin world, ahhh... Oh shit! Free as... ahh muthafucka. Sweetheart, please don't bite my joint."

"Yeah, these young CO's rabid. They love Nesto's dick. Ooh, take it easy. Take it ah... easy, ma. Ma!"

"You know man, I'm thinking ah... yeah... ah yeah ah. I'm thinking of making moves."

"Huh? Ah... oh yeah, oh yeah. What you trying to ah... say Lil' Long? Are you thinking of ah...?"

"I can't ah ooh yeah... talk right nowww!" Lil' Long hummed as the CO's trained tongue slid up and down his hardened shaft. Ernesto stared at him wincing in pleasure.

"Hmm, I thought so." Ernesto's smile widened.

Lil' Long watched as Ernesto indulged in sexual gratification courtesy of the correctional facility. He seemed to enjoy every bit of his stay while locked up. Ernesto had the entire hook up with the Russians. They facilitated all his needs; it was like being on the outside. With his eyes closed, Ernesto grabbed the CO's head and vigorously bobbed it up and down on his dick.

"Yeah, do it ah, yes. That's how you should've been doing it from jump. Oohh!! Agh, agh ugh huh. Yes, take it in your face. Take this cum up in your grill. Oooh, muthafucka. Agh..." Ernesto chuckled.

"Now what were you sayin' to Nesto?

"Agh... yes!" Lil' Long sighed.

"Daddy, daddy you ain't complainin' or sump'n, are you daddy?" Ernesto asked between chuckling.

Lil' Long laughed hard and free before giving a reply.

"Nothing, nada. You know I wasn't complaining for shit dogs."

Nesto pulled his jumpsuit shut and tried to regain his balance.

"Getting my dick blessed makes Nesto fuckin' weak in da knees. You feel me, daddy?"

"Skeetin' all over a bitch's face makes me weak." Lil' Long and Nesto both laughed.

"You heard bout da chess tournament tonight, right?"

"Yeah, you mentioned that bullshit a couple weeks ago."

"That's big 'roun here, daddy. They be havin' that shit once a year. Come through. We'll drink and watch 'em Russians rack up. They ain't lose yet, daddy."

"Oh word? Good I'm definitely gonna have to check on that."

"Ahight, that's good. Nesto will for sure put your name in da books for tonight. You play chess, daddy?"

"A lil' sump'n, sump'n, man. I ain't played that shit in awhile. Matter fact since my man Vulcha been murk, I ain't been fucking with da games. I put all that shit down."

"I hear you, daddy. They got this chess tournament goin' down. Maybe it will be good for you daddy. Them Russians sponsor da shit. They got them CO's playin' too. Daddy, I'm telling you, they bring in expensive ass Russian vodkas by the buckets."

"Damn! Urrh-one be getting' wet then, huh? Ain't nobody escaped?" Lil' Long asked.

"C'mon daddy, don't be a stupid. How you gonna escape and go where?"

"Go da fuck home..." Lil' Long said.

Nesto held up his hand. He put his index finger to his lips.

"Daddy, daddy, round here the walls have ears. You gotta chill with that kinda talk..."

"Whatever man. What about these Russians?"

"Yeah, this Russian dude, Igor and his peeps goes bananas playing any and everyone in this big ass prison tournament of chess. The winners get to drink all this fucking vodka."

"Oh yeah, Igor, your man, he's always winning, huh. Don't sound fair unless someone else wins sometimes. You ever win?"

"Win? Never, Nesto still what you would call a beginner, daddy. I know my place. I'm dead-ass when I say daddy, them Russians got the shit on lock."

"They win all da fucking time?"

"Hell yeah, they nice I'm telling you, daddy. After that, we go get blow-ass on all the fuckin' vodka. They always celebrating, cuz they camp ain't never suffered defeat yet, daddy."

"Don't mean a damn thing 'cept they be ripe for a loss," Lil' Long said rubbing his hands.

"Talk that shit, daddy you gonna have to back it up."

"Ahight, ahight, I'll come check da shit out."

"Daddy, it'll cost you some commissary. Nesto knows you good, so no need to worry 'bout nada," Ernesto smiled.

"Yeah, I'm ahight, but this your world, man," Lil' Long said and lit a cigarette. "I got some shit to settle back in the real world." Nesto nodded at him as if he understood.

"Hey yo Lil' Long man, I got a kite from one o' my boy, Mannie. You know from eastside."

"Muthafuck a kite!" He barked. "I wanna be out there again. Back out in da worl', like a kite. I belong out there, fly like a muthafuckin' pimp. Nesto, man I gotta be back out there holdin' shit down for my Ghetto soldier."

"Daddy, if you talkin' 'bout your man, Vulcha I'm sayin' the Russians can..."

"I don't need no help from no muthafuckin' foreigners. I'm a get at 'em triflin' rappin' ass bitches, that fuckin' music producer all by myself. I got it. Lemme say this, I'm bringing so much fuckin' grief to 'em bitch-asses, them muthafuckas they gon wish they had died the first time aroun'. I'm a hunt they asses down, an' I'm killin' ea-eac-ach o-n-o-one ah-o' th-them!" Lil' Long struggled to get the words out.

Nesto lit a cigarette, puffed and watched Lil' Long furiously pound the wall with his fist. "Hey daddy, be easy..."

"I been easy for too long in this overcrowded muthafuckin' joint. It's time to do my thing. Bust my guns dying. I gotta see 'em muthafuckin' clown ass bitches' smiles turned upside down," Lil' Long yelled.

"Fuck! They whole world up," Ernesto joined in. "Hey Lil' Long you ain't gotta let all that shit bother you, them Russians they have this shit locked. Daddy, daddy I tell you they got some shit they call it bratva."

"And what you tryin' a say, man?" Lil' Long asked.

"I swear on my son's grave, daddy, they like the Italian mob, 'cept twice as deadly. They control every single fuckin' thing on the inside and lots and lots on da fuckin' outside. I'm dead-ass, daddy."

"Oh yeah, you singin' they praises. They real bosses like that?"

"All you gotta do is say the word, daddy an' these niggas will handle shit for you. You my man, daddy and these cats will handle shit. I'm dead-ass, daddy..."

"Nah, I ain't trying to keep no foreign muthafuckas on my dick. I don't need none roun' me. I gotta be back in da hood to do what I do. I'll handle da street shit in da fuckin' streets."

"But daddy, listen to your man Nesto. I'm a put in da word..."

"Nah sun, it ain't happening. I don't need no mo' baggage, muthafucka. I'm a do things my way. Them bosses gonna want tribute on urrh-thing that I do. They just like 'em wop niggas, they all 'bout owning shit. I ain't about to be slingin' for no one like I'm their bitch, a ho or sump'n..."

"All Nesto sayin' is you need to listen to these muthafuckas, they got crazy juice. I'm telling you daddy. Crazy, crazy juice. And they like you."

"Yeah, yeah I hear you, whateva man. I already know what I gotta do to get da fuck up out this joint. And then it's muthafuckin saddle and boots. Ain't no-no-body gonna be sa-sa-afe. I'm a ri-r-ridin' on e-m-m bi-bi-bitches."

"But daddy you could be getting' your hustle on, cuz it's bout da ends. Nesto sayin' it's not gonna hurt to holla at these bratva cats. They got mad plans for the future."

"Fuck all that, man. I'm gonna be out and about, doing what I do, muthafucka. I ain't hatin but I ain't participatin' in da next man plan," Lil' Long said inhaling smoke from his cigarette. His strategy was sewn up. He knew what he had to do.

FOUR

That evening Detective Kowalski and his partner trudged up the stairs to visit Coco at home.

"You have to play good cop. Okay with you Hall. I don't mind locking this smart ass away. I want to scare her first. Maybe she'll open up and talk some. Plus, I know she doesn't care much for me, so she's not going to want to say much to me." Kowalski said as they made it pass the first floor landing.

"You pick the simple ones. Is that it huh?"

"Come on, no faith in the system you rep, partner?"

"No faith? You're always singing about making arrests, tough guy." Hall said as his partner's cell phone rang.

"Hold up," Kowalski said. He looked at his cellphone, smiling from ear to ear. "Let me take this call. I may have turned a snitch," Kowalski said. "Detective Kowalski here operator, go ahead put that call through. So Michael, what's your verdict, guy? Tell me something good, now... It's a simple exchange, you help us in our endeavors and we in return guarantee you freedom. It doesn't take a rocket scientist to recognize a good thing, Michael... But what, Michael? Think about all the good you'll be doing? You'll be helping society get rid of an enemy who's by the way, really trying to kill you. Some ah... coward who put a price on your fucking head, man? Where can you run? We know you want to get back at him for trying to keep you off your turf. We could do a better job of taking him down than you can. We want that big fish worse than you. All you've got to do is say the word and we'll be looking forward to working with you... What's your answer? Gimme a yes and I'll start to work on your freedom immediately, baby. You'll be out so fast."

Kowalski nodded when he heard what he wanted to hear and closed the phone.

He bounded up the stairs ahead of Hall. "How long before Michael Lowe can be released from lock up?" Kowalski asked while his partner stared at him with furrowed brows.

"About seventy-two hours or so why?" Hall asked as they reached the third floor of the building.

"I want him released," Kowalski answered as he examined a fresh bullet hole. "I got the infamous Michael Lowe, alias Lil' Long, cooperating with our team now."

"C'mon, Kowalski, you're still green. Don't get your hopes up too high. You know he's only going along with your plan in order to get out. I don't think he's gonna want to play once he's on the outside."

"There you go again. No faith in the system," Kowalski said looking directly at Hall. "If that piece a shit doesn't cooperate, his ass will be back up in a sling so fast..."

"And what happens if he doesn't want to go back, are

you going to take him out?"

"Believe me, he will have no choice in the matter. It's either give up Eric Ascot or he'll become my bitch on these streets. I'll let everyone of his buddies know he's a faggot and a fucking rat." Kowalski said as he turned to knock on Coco's door. "We're gonna use whatever it takes to break this case wide open. Whatever it takes to make the arrest. You hear me partner?" He banged again on the door. "Where could she go? Didn't the uniform guys tell her to stay put?" Kowalski asked.

"I'm sure they did." Hall deadpanned.

Kowalski knocked loud on the door a few more times. The door next to the apartment opened. Coco peered out.

"Wait a minute. You do not live there. What's this we've got going on here? Is this breaking and entering in progress?" Kowalski asked with sarcasm.

Coco stared at him with a deadly glare before answering. "What do you want? I'm here because Miss Katie is in the hospital and I was about to bring the documents the people at the hospital wanted. So if you don't mind, I'll..."

Kowalski raised his hand. "Don't tell me, you had to break into her apartment to get ah...'The documents?'"

"No, I did not break-in. I have Miss Katie's keys."

"Oh you do?"

"If you did your homework you'd know that Miss Katie has been taking care of me since..."

"Since your mother has been in drug rehab," Detective Hall said.

"Okay what's your point? You know everything. So can

I go about my bidness now?" She asked as impolite as possible.

"Why don't you talk to us? Is there a reason why you do not trust the police? We are here to protect and serve..." Hall said.

"You ain't protecting or serving me..."

"Young lady, couple weeks ago we could've arrested you for loitering in a drug infested area. The place where you were caught we know for certain that if you're anywhere in that vicinity, you're there for one reason only, and that's to buy drugs. Now we did not arrest you, we did not even search you, which if we did, we'd probably found a bag or two of that reefer..."

"Huh? What reefer? What're you talkin' about? C'mon, I don't use no reefer."

"What do you use Coco?" The detective asked.

Coco slowly shook her head.

"Huh, I didn't hear you?" The detective asked.

"Look I don't be... the most I smoke is cigarettes..." Coco started to respond. She became suspicious and her voice trailed off.

"Where do you buy the cigarettes?" Hall asked.

"Yeah, I wanna hear this one," Kowalski said with a smirk.

"I bum smokes off people, ahight. When my mother is home I be borrowing off her."

"How old are you?" Hall asked.

"You know everything else, you should know my age."

"She's only seventeen..." Kowalski said.

"It's just about illegal for you to do anything, Coco." Hall interrupted.

"So...?"

"Please, let's go inside your apartment. We'd like to talk to you about the gunshots that were fired earlier." Neighbors started slowly easing out of their apartments into the hallway.

"Look, why can't we talk about this another time, yo? I already spoke to the other police about that. I mean I gotta go to the hospital and take them these documents," Coco complained as she opened the door to her mother's apartment. She entered and the detectives followed.

"Hmm, new furniture." Kowalski walked in and immediately surveyed the room.

"Okay young lady, tell us what happened," Hall demanded in a comforting fatherly tone.

"Earlier? Ahight, ahight already, this girl attacked some other girl when she got off the elevator."

"What caused the attack?" Hall asked. While sitting facing Hall, Coco's eyes never let Kowalski out of her vision. He was strolling around the room examining things.

"Coco, do you know what caused the attack on the girl?" Hall repeated.

"I don't know. Maybe they didn't like the fact that her gears was better than theirs, or sump'n," Coco answered sarcastically.

"A gun was fired. Do you know who fired the gun?" Hall asked.

"I don't know."

"Any idea? You were close enough," Hall said.

"Yeah, but understand, you in the hood, and ain't nobody sticking around trying to see if someone pulled out a gun. You be out, running, or you ducking, man," Coco added with a shrug.

"If it was all running and ducking, how do you know someone had a gun?" Hall asked.

"One of them did. Sump'n went bang. Someone let off but I'm damn Skippy, it wasn't me. And that's what's really up."

"Is that your story?"

"*My story*? That's what happened."

"We spoke to several people who suggested that maybe you also had a gun. Or..." Hall began to say.

Coco walked to the door and opened it. She stuck her head out and yelled:

"People round here need to learn to mind their damn BI and stop giving po-po wrong info, yo." She slammed the door then returned to face Hall.

"You're being straight with us, Coco? You are aware that you can go to jail for a very long time for lying to the police." Hall said.

"I don't know what you're talkin' bout, yo."

"C'mon Coco give us a name. You're a smart girl, I'm sure you know one name," Hall pleaded.

Kowalski walked over closer to them. His face bore an agitated look of impatience. He stood in front of Coco trying to intimidate her.

"Yeah, why won't you give us the right info, huh?" He asked. Before Coco could give an answer, Kowalski moved closer. He continued yelling in her face. "You lied about your involvement in Ascot's shooting. I'll bet anything that you're lying about your attackers and who had the guns. You're covering up your involvement in each of these instances and I don't like it one bit."

"She told us whatever she knew," Hall offered weakly in Coco's defense. "We can't blame her, she had to duck. Bullets have no names on them. You know, you got to get out the way..."

"I don't believe a thing this lying Black bitch has said so far!" Kowalski screamed. Coco bit her lips and clenched her fist.

"Hey man, be easy now. You can't be just going around making racial slurs..." Hall cautioned.

"I could give a rat's ass about race. We are here to catch criminals."

"But she's not a criminal," Hall said trying to no avail to step between his partner and Coco.

Kowalski was so close to Coco that the spatter of his saliva sprinkled her face. She turned to wipe it off.

"I'm going to prove that you're nothing but a liar Coco. You break the damn law, you smoke your weed, drink your alcohol, you think that is so cool. You and your friends were probably coming back here to smoke this," he said holding a bag of weed close to her surprised face. "Someone lost the bag when a fight broke out. I am here investigating a crime and found a bag laying in plain view inside your apartment. Marijuana is illegal. Your ass is grass, Coco. I'm gonna be that lawnmower and cut you down."

Coco glanced at it and smirked. It was a dub sack, the type she never bought. This incident made her remember the social workers; they had found another bag of weed a couple weeks ago.

"If your jail-bait-ass does not come clean right here and now, the sounds you're gonna hear is cling-cling on your way down to the poky." Kowalski roared as if he had won.

Coco shook her head. She opened her mouth but nothing came. In the back of her mind, she could hear her mother's voice screaming: '*You were smoking weed in my apartment?*'

"What other lies do you have for us, Coco?"

"That isn't mine," she said trying to convince herself more so than the detectives. "You both know that it's not. You did not smell any marijuana in here. What're you trying to do?" Coco screamed. "You're trying to frame me for sump'n I ain't do. I never fired no gun. I don't even own a gun. Why y'all don't go harass the person who fired the gun? And stop tryin' to plant weed on me."

"What's her name, Coco?" Kowalski asked hypnotically shaking the bag side to side in Coco's face.

"I don't know. Why you fuckin' with me? I ain't no rat. I ain't gonna be snitching out anyone I don't know."

"Oh well, lil' sis it's gonna be your behind. There won't be a lot that I can do to stop this racist cop from arresting you and sending you to jail for a long time." Hall said.

"She's wasting my time. Let's go!" Kowalski said gruffly shaking his handcuffs. He approached Coco with his handcuffs undone.

"You can't arrest me! Why you gonna?" Coco was out-raged.

"Because we represent the law and you've broken it, Coco. You're under arrest for possession of marijuana," Kowalski said. Coco shoved him when he tried to put the hand-cuffs on her wrists. "Now you're resisting arrest. I'll gladly add that to your charges."

"Coco, don't make things any worse," Hall stated.

"Bitch, put your hands behind you," Kowalski ordered. "Do you have anything in your pockets that is gonna stab me, any pointed objects or a knife?" He yelled slapping the hand-cuffs onto Coco's wrists.

She was on the floor with Kowalski's knees on her neck.

"Ugh... No," Coco said barely audible. Suddenly she felt Hall hands rifling through the pockets of her jeans. Coco bit her lips and tears welled in her eyes as she allowed him to frisk her. She shifted her hands and felt the handcuffs tightened on her wrists when Kowalski jerked her to her feet.

"Let's go. This bag of weed is going to send your black ass directly to jail," Kowalski growled. "You have the right to remain silent. Anything you say may and will be used against you..."

Coco tried to erase the words from her mind. She walked in front, her head low as the detectives led her through the hallway and out of the building.

"Coco, please watch your head." Hall ordered as he neatly stuffed Coco in the back seat of the black Caprice.

"All aboard!" Kowalski humorously announced from the

driver's seat. "Here's your free ride to jail, bitch." Kowalski laughed.

"Take it easy you crazy cop!" Hall said to Kowalski.

FIVE

That evening in the recreation area of the correctional facility, Lil' Long was one of the many onlookers watching a game of chess between Ernesto and one of his muscled Russian comrades. They were all from Eastern Europe and all had flying dragons tattooed on their huge chests. Sensing that they were waiting to cheer for the big Russian, Lil' Long chuckled when Nesto fell to a simple but well executed move by the Russian champ.

"Ah, it's this Russian blood I tell you Nesto. I cannot be defeated," the Russian laughed and hugged Ernesto. "That's about two cartons of Marlboro, my boy."

"I got next," Lil' Long shouted. The Russian looked up, smiled and with a wave of his muscular arm welcomed Lil' Long to sit as the next challenger at the table. Ernesto got up and slapped Lil' Long a dap.

"Lil' Long this man is good. Good luck, the loser pays for

a bottle of Vodka and two cartons. It's some expensive shit." Ernesto whispered to Lil' Long who was now in the process of taking the vacated seat.

"You understand the rules of the game? Think before you give your answer. I want you to know that I'm playing to win," the Russian said.

"I ain't played in a minute, but me an' my man..." Lil' Long's voice trailed off.

"But you can play, can't you?" The Russian asked eagerly. "Ha, ha, surely you remember something about the game? I don't wanna keep beating novices."

"I got your novice right here," Lil' Long stared at the pieces and smiled.

"In a short while, we drink some real Vodka," he bragged to a small crowd made large by their muscles. "I will have this win in a couple of quick moves. Friends watch carefully and learn. This is a brave man."

"I wish my man Vulcha was here to witness this," Lil' Long said glancing at the confused faces around him. "You da champ make your move." Lil' Long said.

Lil' Long stared in the Russian's eyes and quickly realized his strategy was to use a pawn to make way for his queen. Then put the opposition's king in check. Trapped, the king would be forced into checkmate by the opposing bishop or rook. Lil' Long moved a pawn to block the Russian's attempt at ending the chess match early.

"Oh I see, you have understanding of game," the Russian smiled as he moved his bishop into attack mode.

Lil' Long countered with a knight neutralizing the

Russians move and putting him on the defensive. As the match wore on, themes of strategy became blurred and for the most part the direction of the game seemed obscured. Lil' Long thrived in the confusion.

The boastful Russian realized that the young street thug had a sophisticated defense strategy, which lulled him in a false sense of security. Before he was conceitedly finished with his explanation of Sputnik, Lil' Long had gained the upper hand.

The defending champion dodged and hid his pieces in a vain attempt at retreat. His execution was less than flawless. He had failed to connect Lil' Long's tactic from the opening to the middle of the match. The street warrior threw chaotic planned attacks. He sent a message that made his opponent pay for his aggressive beginning by sacrificing pawns to disguise his attacks on the ultimate prize.

They traded and counter-traded unimportant pieces and neither backed down. Black faces were now prominent in the crowd that gathered. Everyone fell silent and held their collective breaths when they heard Lil' Long confidently make a decisive call.

"Check," he barked. It came like a jolt of electricity and made the Russian sit up straight. His proud mind attempted to fathom the depth of his trouble. He scanned the chessboard analyzing his next move. He had none. The street thug had outplayed him. Since coming to this correctional facility ten years ago, he had never lost a chess match.

"That makes it checkmate, my sputnik," Lil' Long laughed. Everyone in the recreation area breathed with a collective sigh.

The Russian did not look up.

"What's your name? Beginners luck? I want a rematch," he demanded and looked at Lil' Long. "I'll double any wager."

"I'll grant you that rematch but what if you lose. We ain't gonna be playin' all muthafuckin' night, is we?"

"Everywhere I go, the people around know me as Igor. I'm a very fair man and a man of my word," the Russian said reaching his hand to shake Lil' Long's. "Go ahead, it's your move."

The buzz of the audience ceased when Lil' Long made his move. The Russian studied the board while sweating with intensity. He realized that Lil' Long was on the offense from the jump. He countered.

There were additional inmates taking bets. As the betting pool widened the Russian was odds-on favorite to win. Most figured Lil' Long would be unable to beat the Russian a second time. All eyes stayed glued to the movement of the chess pieces on the board.

Both players tested each other's defenses. Lil' Long knew a big moment had arrived as he held the king in position and made the call. His opponent realized too late that Lil' Long had set this attack as far back as his first move.

"Check," Lil' Long said with fierceness.

"Check," the big Russian countered after vigorously moving pieces around. Igor knew his king was in trouble and needed to buy time. He attempted a routine blocking move, but the Lil' Long was undaunted in his efforts and relentlessly attacked until there was hush along the sidelines.

"Checkmate, muthafucka!"

A loud roar erupted from the crowd. The brothers gath-ered threw high fives all the way around as Lil' Long snickered in his victory. This brought smiles to the faces of even the meanest correction officers. Igor stared in astonishment at the board.

"I'm a man of my word, Lil' Long. I 'll pay tribute with some of the finest vodka in the world," the Russian said.

He directed Lil' Long away from the table and the other inmates who had gathered. "Come with me. Let's go. We will play again, soon."

"No doubt you'll have another rematch." Lil' Long said as he walked along side the Russian.

"Tell me where did you learn to play so well?"

"What, it's been about like six years ago when I was first locked down. This CO showed me how to move the pieces around, you know? Long story short, I just kept playin', devel-opin' my own muthafuckin' strategies. Ya feel me?"

"Ha, ha, and here you are, new champion." Igor handed Lil' Long a large glass. "So the CO's do have some use, huh?"

There was an echo of laughter and it was then that Lil' Long realized all the others who were in tow. The entire Russian posse consisted of three body builders plus Ernesto was sticking close.

"I hope your country have tha good shit..." Lil' Long offered but the Russian held his hand to stop him.

"I assure you it's absolutely the best," the Russian said and they all moved on. His cell was well kept. It even had car-pet and a Phillips LCD monitor to watch cable television.

"Y'all muthafuckas sick wit it in here, dogs," Lil' Long

announced surveying the space.

The Russian whispered and with a snap of his fingers, cigars and vodka appeared. They raised their glasses, drank and toasted a couple rounds. Lil' Long glad-handed with the Russians.

He understood this type of protection and knew it came with a huge price tag attached.

"Something tells me you want to leave here. You don't like it here at our facility?" Igor asked.

"In here is all good for y'all but I got things, I got some BI I gotta handle back on da street. You feel me?" Lil' Long said.

"This ah, BI is it enough to make you want to cooperate with the law?" Igor asked.

Lil' Long stared at the muscular Russian who was wearing a smile. Then lunged at him, but a large boot tripped him. He fell to the rug. Before Lil' Long could recover, three other muscular bodies dove on top of him. They smothered him. One pulled out a shank.

"Nyet, not yet, comrade. Let's work with this man. He has spunk and despite the odds, he would rather die than give up. Am I correct with the assessment, Mr. Long?"

When Lil' Long was dragged to his feet, he stood face to face with the Russian. Lil' Long bit his lips.

"So what's your beef bout, man? I don't care what 'cha know, ma-m-m-man!" Lil' Long said.

Nesto kept a close eye on him. He whispered something to the Russian.

"Listen and you're gonna have to learn to do exactly what you're told to do. Or else..." Igor started.

"Or else what man?" Lil' Long challenged. The Russian lit a cigar and puffed before he answered.

"Or else nothing goes on. You're going to come to understand that nothing goes on without my say so. Not a family visit, a walk to the yard, use of the recreation room. Nothing goes down unless I okay it. You will pay tribute for the privilege of leaving here."

"What da fuck are you going on about, man?" Lil' Long asked. "Who da fuck you think you are?" He wondered aloud.

"My name is Igor Daks and everyone reports to me. I have connections on the inside and the outside wherever you go." Igor paused puffing on his cigar. He exhaled in Lil' Long's face, looked the street thug up and down before continuing.

"I want you to handle your so-called BI, Mr. Long but I've got a proposal for you. You'll see it's quite a simple one with lots and lots of returns for both of us."

Igor smiled and puffed on his cigar then exhaled. Lil' Long looked around the well-furnished prison cell, exhaled then sat down on a sofa. He smoked, sipped and listened while trying to contain his rage.

SIX

Coco sat uneasy on the hard bench. She rubbed her back, which ached from sitting in the same position for over three hours. She turned her head toward the ceiling and whispered a prayer for Miss Katie. She was distracted by the parade of usual suspects in central booking, as white officers of the law hauled young Blacks and Latinos in.

She watched fiends squabbled for the disgustingly stale bologna and cheese sandwiches.

"You come with me," a uniformed officer ordered.

Coco struggled to her feet, stretched, and walked away with him. He led her to a room and sat her down alone. Moments later the door swung open. Kowalski and Hall strolled in.

"Coco my girl, how're you doing yo?" Kowalski asked in mocking tones.

He had a huge smile waiting to pop like a zit on his face. Hall laughed. Coco scowled and with a frown, Kowalski began baiting Coco. Hall got between them.

"Why don't you want to cooperate with the law? You see us as being weak?" Hall demanded.

"I wanna speak to a lawyer. Are you gonna deny me my rights?" Coco asked.

Kowalski paced, fuming, pointing and yelling at Coco.

"Rights? You have no rights. You're better off throwing yourself on the mercy of the court. A bag of weed and you gave up all your so-called rights. It looks like you're going to meet big mama, girlfriend."

Hall pleaded with Coco. "Maybe you should reconsider. Any information that you provide us with may help someone from being murdered again. Ascot's involvement is the key to this investigation. You're going to save yourself and your mother a lot of headaches of dealing with the system. I mean the simplest thing for you to do is help us solve these murders and you're free."

"You're gonna be locked away for a while. You're going to do some time. Time you can rap about," Kowalski said pointing his finger at her. "My partner, he thinks your life may just be worth a French flying rat's ass. Frankly, I don't care. It doesn't make a difference. I know if you don't cooperate then you're going down with all of them, Eric Ascot and all his mob cronies."

"I'm not saying one more thing until y'all let me speak to a lawyer. I know my rights," she said and began humming softly.

The detectives looked quizzically at each other.

"Coco, if you don't stop behaving like a retard right now, your ass will go to jail and your mother..." Kowalski started.

Coco hummed loud enough to drown out his voice.

The detectives walked out the room and left the teenager alone for a brief period. Coco was still humming when they returned. This time they were accompanied by a uniformed officer.

"All right this officer is here to process you unless you got something to share with us," Kowalski announced. "You can go to jail for up to eighteen months on a charge of possession of narcotics."

"Maybe I can speak to her alone," Hall said and took a notepad from the uniformed officer. The others exited the room. "Let me tell you that I have children, your age even. My son is just two years older than you are."

"Then you should understand that I don't wanna be here, I wanted to visit with someone who's close to me. She's in the hospital and y'all got..."

"Coco, first thing first, there was a bag of marijuana found in a place you occupied. Now the fact is we could just stick you in a jail cell. We're trying to help you open your eyes. You have information on a case involving the death of a police officer. In addition, well, my crazy partner thinks you're holding back on key info. Now I told him you're not. He's dreaming. The fact is Coco, I'm trying to prevent you from going to jail and he's trying to send you there as an accessory to murder. You'll be guaranteed to live the rest of your life locked up behind bars because the lives of two police officers were taken."

"I don't know about anything like that, yo. Y'all are tryin' to pin sump'n I ain't do. I ain't scared."

"Now, now the simplest thing would be, if you have anything you might want to say, just tell him what you know and... If you don't want to speak with either of us, then I'm begging you, urging you, encouraging you to write down what you know on this notepad and I'll witness your signature," Hall said handing a notepad to Coco.

She glanced at it with disdain.

"If you're not comfortable," Hall continued. "I mean if for some reason you don't want to write..."

"Look all this BS act, you could just save, ahight. I know you're just trying to get me to speak on things I don't know nothing about..."

"No that's not true, Coco. You were witness to a shooting and the gun used is the same gun used to kill a police officer..."

"I didn't kill anyone why don't you go out and find the real killer and harass them?" Coco screamed with tears streaming down her face.

Hall waited, put the notepad down then he offered her tissue for her tears.

"That's exactly what we're trying to do but we need your help, Coco. Anything you give us, or think of would help us tremendously. Of course, this means you'd also be helping yourself. I'm telling you right now, you do not want that crazy white boy charging you as an accessory to murder. He wants to lock you away for the rest of your life. Now, you know fully well that is a very heavy, heavy weight to carry. Especially when you weren't personally involved. Think about it Coco, I am trying to help you out as best I can, Coco. Take some time to think about it. He hates black people."

Detective Hall got up from the small table. He left the blank notebook on the desk in front of Coco.

"I'm gonna go out and try to calm my partner. He just wants to throw you in jail. I wanna help you do the right thing." On his way out the room, Hall turned to Coco. "Can I get you something to drink, water?"

Coco heard the door slam. She did not take her eyes off the blank notepad.

SEVEN

Deedee turned off the television and picked up her cell phone checking for messages from Coco. It was two-thirty in the morning and Deedee was wide-awake when she hit the redial button. She listened to the outgoing message on Miss Katie's answering machine. She waited patiently for the extended beep.

"Yo Coco, this is Dee. Hit me when you get this. Let me know you're okay and how Miss Katie is doing."

It was the fourth or fifth message she had left since yesterday. She also tried sending text messages to Coco but there was no response. She felt tired but sleep would not come.

Since arriving home, Deedee had Coco and Miss Katie on her mind. She explained the incident to her uncle's fiancée, Sophia, who had long since retired to bed. She told Sophia how scary things got when the girl pulled out the gun, but Sophia seemed uninterested. She only suggested that Deedee stay away from the area and take out an order of protection against the girls. The advice was curt but Deedee didn't mind.

She knew that Sophia was more concerned with her situation with Eric than high school girls fighting.

Deedee's mind was still on the incident when the ringing of the phone startled her. She rushed to get it.

"Hello, Josephine." Deedee said flatly.

"It's Coco. She hasn't called since I left her some hours ago... No, Jo, earlier me and Coco and these girls... the same girls who had a fight with you, well we were kicking their asses and one of them pulled out a gun and fired a shot... Jo, Miss Katie was outside and... I don't think so, but she was laid out in the hallway when I left. And Coco was supposed to call me after they got to the hospital, but I haven't heard from her yet."

Josephine was crying on the other end of the line. Deedee felt something else had drawn Josephine's wailing.

"How're things going so far with you and your mother?" Deedee asked warily. "I'm sorry to hear that y'all fighting again... Jo, if you want you could come here and live maybe finish school and... Let me know and I'll make the arrangements, okay... Bye."

Deedee sat up in bed, thinking about the conversation. She knew she would need her uncle's approval for Josephine to stay. She dialed his number. He picked up after the third ring.

"Uncle E., I hate to be bothering you but I just wanna know if I can have a friend stay with us for the semester, maybe? It's ah... Josephine. She and her parents are going through a bad divorce and she can't concentrate in school... That'll be good Uncle. She'll be happy to know. When am I gonna see you? Dinner at seven sounds good... and yes I'll get a note to her parents so that she can legitimately enroll in school... Wow Uncle, you're always in the studio working and... you almost live there. Anyway I'll see you later."

Deedee turned off the lights, laid on the bed and stared at the ceiling until she fell asleep.

EIGHT

Monday morning started with spatters of rain carried over from the previous night. The early morn air felt crisp against Rachel Harvey's face as she dashed out of the cab. She ran through the entrance of the building without stopping. When she was about to open the door to her apartment she realized that she had left her luggage in the trunk of the cab.

She hesitated for a moment but was sure the cabdriver would be long gone. Once she entered the apartment she was immediately stunned by the new furniture she momentarily forgot everything except concern for her daughter. She picked up some papers and made her way out of the renovated apartment. She hailed a cab. "Center Street, please."

Rachel Harvey walked nervously to join a queue outside the courthouse. She went through the metal detector.

"I'm here for my daughter..." she said clearing a lump in her throat. The officer pointed to another section.

"Wait over there you'll hear her name called," he said.

Rachel Harvey nervously ambled over to a crowded waiting area. She searched for a seat. It was standing room only. A few minutes later, she spotted a group of new releases celebrating their departure. She scrambled to get a seat, sat and shook her legs nervously while she waited. After an anxious hour had gone by, Rachel caught a glimpse of her daughter speaking to another person. Her heart sank when she noticed the handcuff on her. She waved when the officer led Coco into the courtroom.

Another hour went by before Mrs. Harvey was called. The officer directed her inside the courtroom. There were people everywhere. By the time she had made it through the throngs of family members and attorneys, the teenage defendant and her attorney were already standing in front of the Judge. She rushed to her daughter's side.

"And you are?" The judge paused and asked.

"I'm her mother, your honor."

"State your name and the relationship to the child for the record," the court officer said.

"My name is Rachel Harvey. I'm Coco's mother."

"The lawyer assigned will explain all the details to you," the judge said to Mrs. Harvey before addressing Coco. "Young lady, you're being given twelve months probation. If for any reason you return to this court within that period, then I'll re-rule. Probation granted. Good luck." He said and struck the gavel against the bench.

"Party's free to go," the court officer yelled. "Next case State verses Jones..."

Coco and her mother were ushered into a small room by

the attorney.

"She has to go to school and back home everyday. She'll have to see someone in probation before she leaves," the attorney said while signing document after document and shoving each at Mrs. Harvey. "Ah, good luck... ah Coco. I have to go. Dozens of cases," she said flying out the door.

Mrs. Harvey looked around the office shaking her head in disbelief.

"Why, Coco? Can you tell me why?"

Coco did not respond. Her lips went dry thinking of where to begin.

"You're not gonna open your mouth now, huh? Tell me why you wanna be a thug girl instead of a lady. I'm trying to raise you right Coco..."

The door opened and an officer peered inside.

"You're needed right away in the probation office. All the offices are downstairs."

NINE

"I don't understand. What's the problem with the fucking release papers?" Kowalski yelled into the phone. He hung up, threw the papers down, and marched angrily from his desk. On his way out the precinct, he saw his partner standing at the vending machines reading a report.

"What does one have to do around here to get things done?" Kowalski complained.

Hall looked him up and down for a beat before he answered. "You look like shit. Maybe you should first address your wardrobe. Look your appearance is way too shoddy. I don't even know where to begin..."

"Be careful of what you about to say, man. I'm not in the mood..."

"Feeling froggie white-boy?"

"No, all I'm trying to do is make a damn case. A major case that the damn chief himself wants wrapped up as soon as possible. It's next to impossible to get any type of cooperation around here. I need to arrest someone... anyone."

"Let's go get some real coffee and assess our situation," Hall said. "Now first, when making a case stick, you're only as good as your witness. We don't have such a..."

"I've got a good connection," Kowalski said interrupting Hall.

"Who do you have?" Hall asked choosing the Cappuccino flavor from a vending machine that was a few feet from the first one.

"Lil' Long..." Kowalski began.

"You have nothing."

"What're you saying?"

"There are plenty of people mad at him. He has far too many enemies. The cost is going to be too heavy, and that's just to begin to work with him." Hall cautioned and sipped.

"Well what do we have then?"

"We've got someone like Rightchus out on the streets and free just waiting for someone to turn him on."

"Rightchus? A drugged out piece-o'-shit for brains?"

"Yes, that's the one. Let's pay him a visit and I'll explain further."

"What does Lil' Long pissing a bunch a people off has to do with our investigation?" Kowalski asked.

"You're on your own on that one. But my guess is these people must be very powerful, because all of a sudden they are turning their backs on him," Hall answered.

"Let's go see your man, Rightchus. Then drop in and see

our shooter, Tina Torres. She called to give us insight as to what had happened," Kowalski said.

TEN

Lil' Long sat on his bunk staring at the puke on the four walls that had him penned. Since meeting the Russian he knew his list of enemies was growing longer. He jumped up and paced the cell as Ernesto entered.

"What da fuck you here for?" Lil' Long growled.

"Easy daddy, you sound like you mad at Nesto."

"What, you come up in here for? You da muthafuckin' enforcer or sump'n, Nesto? Tell me what you be about, man?"

"Look, daddy I told you that anything that goes on in here is sanctioned by the Russians. This prison bidness, they own it and we existing under their rules, daddy."

"Whatcha mean, man? What da fuck is you talkin' bout?"

"I'm dead ass, the prison system has been privatized for a minute, daddy. This a private joint, they got you locked down in, daddy."

"Huh what man, wha' da fuck you sayin?'"

"To put it simple, there are these guys who own the joint, daddy. They own where we now residing."

"And fuckin' what?"

"Just hear me out, daddy. Bidness men own the jails, daddy and they peeps in here, and they running things. You smell me daddy? They set all the rules. Not the department of corrections or whateva, fuck that shit, daddy, they only lease the name. Nothing happens without the people running things say so. You feel me now?"

"You sayin' these muthafuckin Russians and they peeps be on some landlord and tenants type shit?"

"That's it in a nutshell, daddy. You come up in here you gotta pay rent daddy."

"Oh, so who da fuck you be? A fuckin' rent collector or sump'n?"

"Nah, daddy, Nesto ain't nothing like that," Ernesto said with a laugh. "Nesto being real with you, daddy, like you being real with Nesto. You feel me? You know this chick Tina, daddy?"

Lil' Long watched carefully as Ernesto pulled out a wrapped object. He jumped toward him. The muscular man easily pushed Lil' Long off.

"C'mon daddy, if Nesto wanted to shank you, I wouldn't have to do a damn thing, 'cept say the word, daddy. It would be over for you daddy," Nesto said lining up the pure white in Lil' Long's view. He snorted in both nostrils then looked over at Lil' Long.

"Hmm... Nah, I'm good, man. So I ain't gonna leave

unless I cooperate with em Russians, huh?"

"Daddy they run shit, right now. When we sit down again I'm a show you some science behind their whole shit. Right now Nesto gotta go get that weight training on."

"Leave me some o' that Columbian white, ahight."

"No problem, daddy. This shit ain't free though, daddy. This gonna cost you some commissary."

"Whateva, man. You know I got that," Lil' Long said watching Ernesto pull out the wrapped object then throwing the plastic bag across the cell.

Lil' Long readied himself by pouring the coke out. As soon as he was about to snort the white powder, he felt a blow upside his head.

"Take this snitch!"

Dazed he struggled to see who his attackers were. Two or three stayed around and kicked him.

"Don't hurt him, he da muthafucking chess champin..."

"Die! Muthafuckin' you rat!" They yelled.

Lil' Long was dragged by the seat of his pants into the hall where he was given another beating.

He was wallowing in pain as he slowly regained consciousness. He struggled to his feet. The CO came, confiscated the coke and dragged him to the hole.

"I ain't done shit!" Lil' Long yelled, as he was shoved into the darkened hole.

ELEVEN

It was early in the afternoon. Coco and her mother sat in a cramped office trying to maintain poise. They had been waiting for what felt like the entire day. A parole officer walked in for a minute, picked up papers off his desk and left silently. He repeated the cycle of suddenly appearing, remaining for a short time and then leaving without saying anything.

The distraught teen glanced away trying not to look at her mother.

"Hurry-up and wait, that's all they seem to do 'round here. This is just another way they get on your damn nerve and it's all your damn fault Coco. You really over-did yourself welcoming me home this time. What was you thinking, Coco? Haven't you learned anything?" Rachel Harvey asked her silent daughter. "It's like all I done did to keep your ass from hard times, is da more you tryin' to go there. I'll end it for you Coco. I tried to keep you out da shelter system. You know these people they could take you off da budget and put me up in da shelter. An' I ain't goin' to live under 'em conditions, cuz when you become shelterized you get used to people pissing all over you."

"Shelterized?" Coco repeated softly.

"Yes, that's when you don't go to school and give up all your hopes. Your dreams vanish soon you in a shelter. I don't wanna become shelterized and I damn well don't want you to go that route. But, I can only suggest that to you Coco, cuz you soo damn grown. You know everything. I'm telling you one thing, you better do whatever these people ask you to do or else that judge will send your behind to the damn slammer."

Coco, closemouthed, looked straight ahead, trying not to make eye contact with her mother's angry scowl. A little after that Ward made another unannounced entrance to his office. He followed the same actions as before, except this time he spoke to the parent and child in front of him.

"Good afternoon. My name is PO Ward and I will supervise your release. Now as a probationer..."

"I thought I was on...?" Coco asked confused.

"The next time you disturb me when I'm speaking, you'll be that much closer to going inside. Good manners and respect are the most important tools for all my probationers. Respect others and you'll be given respect. When someone is speaking, especially someone who is in authority such as your mother, or a person like myself, you must listen carefully and wait until that person is finished speaking before you say anything. Do you understand what I'm saying, Miss Coco Harvey?"

Coco mumbled inaudibly.

"I can't hear you? What did you say?"

"I hear you, I understand." Coco said.

"Now you're here for rehab of a particular drug problem."

"Coco you have a drug problem? Is that whatcha doing? Is you a druggie now, Coco?" Rachel Harvey screamed in dismay. "What, I go for treatment and you think you can go get hooked on what you feel like, huh?"

"Mrs. Harvey, Mrs. Harvey please, I would like to address this matter right now. I'm sure you'll have time later to discipline your daughter. Coco, you'll be coming to see me every Tuesday evening after school at four-thirty. That gives you enough time to finish all your classes and be in here on time. Not on cp time, or your time, it will be my time. Do you understand?" Ward asked.

Coco nodded.

"Any questions let me know now. I don't want to hear the excuse that you didn't understand anything I said. I'll explain it all again if I have to. Your curfew will be at seven, every day. That means if for any reason you're caught outside your home, your place of domicile after seven, then it is a violation and you're subject to being arrested. Do you understand? I want you to speak up. I can't understand you, so I want to hear you say yes I understand or no I don't understand."

"Yes, I understand."

"What's my name?"

"Ah... Officer Ward."

"PO Ward, Miss."

"Okay..."

"Also because you were found with marijuana in your

possession and I gathered some information that this is not the first time marijuana has been found on you by a city official."

"Huh?" Mrs. Harvey blurted.

"Seems like a week ago, a caseworker found a similar bag of weed at your home. Of course, that matter is going to be handled by another department. But because you were found with an illegal drug in connection to a criminal investigation, you'll have to participate in a drug treatment program. A female officer will supervise all the testing of your urine and I'll make the necessary determination. On your next visit, I'll have the name of a program for you. Are there any questions? Since there are no questions, Coco come with me."

Mrs. Harvey got up but Ward waved her off by raising his arm. "I'll be back to tell you your responsibility. Just give me a second."

TWELVE

That evening Deedee's uncle picked her up from school. A beefy bodyguard who doubled as his driver accompanied him. Deedee climbed into the backseat where her uncle was busy putting away loads of papers. He appeared worn and there was a three-day growth of hair on his face. She knew he had been busy all day and night. Eric often worked for days without any rest developing music.

"Hey Dee, how're you hon?" He greeted her with a kiss on the cheek.

"Hi Uncle E. How was your day?" Deedee asked returning the affection.

"Crazy, I spent all day laying down some tracks."

"Were they the same ones you were working on last night?"

"Right, I did talk to you like late, after midnight, right?"

"Yes you did. I called because I couldn't sleep."

"You must be feeling a little tired then."

"Somewhat, but I'll be alright. How did the session come off?"

"It turned out to be more. See I didn't want to be too fancy, that was part of the manager's instructions. Nothing too fancy. I prepared some you know, generic R&B stuff. Then the group showed up and was feeling all the Hip Hop stuff. So I had to reset everything. That really took me out of it. Felt like I was doing everything except licking the stamp today."

"Yeah, that really sounds like a lot on your plate, Uncle. I guess you had a full day."

"Yeah, but right now, we're gonna have a nice filet mignon at Tuscan Steak."

"Hmm, sounds great. I like. That should revive you, huh Uncle."

"Hope so, I hope so, Dee. How about you, how was your day, sweetheart?"

"I'm afraid no better than yours, Uncle E. I spent the day waiting for Coco to call but she hasn't yet."

"Why, what's up with Coco?"

"Oh, I hope nothing, just that she wasn't at school."

"I thought she wanted to get into a good college?"

"Yeah, but I don't know. Anyway, I picked up homework for her to do. She's serious about school and I know it had to be really, really serious for her to miss school today."

Deedee looked over at her uncle next to her. His eyes were shut. Deedee stopped speaking and leaned back closing her eyes also.

Later the two took their places inside the popular steak house.

Eric finished his meal, sipped a glass of beer and watched his niece giving him furtive glances while nursing her apple pie.

"How was your meal?" He asked.

Deedee smiled

"It was really good. I just couldn't eat it all. Uncle are you and..." Deedee paused and looked at her uncle before continuing.

"What is the matter hon?"

"It's just that I was thinking you should ah... take a vacation and maybe invite Sophia..." Deedee started and slowed as she saw the contortions of her uncle's brows. "Like maybe you need time from your daily grind just to breathe and you may at the same time invite Sophia. Then you guys could spend... you know? Like a week, together communicating and maybe you can work things out. Uncle, please consider what I'm saying."

"Dee, listen I don't know how much of your attention you should give to this kind of adult mess. You just got to make sure everything goes right with your graduation from high school. Then you've got college. Graduating was what your father wanted for you to do. He wanted you to reach your potential, not be involved with things like Soph and me, that's grown folks biz..."

"But Uncle I see her and I know..."

"Dee, remember when I used to take you to those karate lessons. Well this is what all that training was for, so you can be disciplined enough to forget all this negative around you and focus on your scholastic goals."

"Yeah, but Uncle Sophia misses you too."

Her uncle swallowed the rest of his beer as Deedee continued.

"You guys should try to work on it and not try to ignore each other's existence. You bury yourself in music and Sophia's trying to hide her tears from the world by sitting in front of her computer..."

"Dee," Eric said raising his hand. "Look, I gave her the best jewelry from Harry Winston. I ordered her favorite car, the Porsche Boxter and had it delivered. I've sent flowers to her job and home on a regular. Since the whole thing went down, I've spent money buying so many trinkets for Sophia that..." Eric struggled for a moment. "C'mon for heavens sake, she doesn't even wear her engagement ring anymore. Dee, love's a two way street and for it to work, the other person got to meet you half way."

"You're right, Uncle E., maybe if I talk to her maybe if you offered her San Tropez for a week, maybe I could sort of feel her out..."

"Exactly not the thing I want you to do. She's gonna assume that I'm using you to get at her. I want her to see that we're all humans and anyone can make a mistake. I made my fair share, but that doesn't mean I'm the scum of the earth. At the moment Sophia's intelligence is telling her that's just what I am."

THIRTEEN

Coco stood in front of the window in the kitchen looking down at the streets. She saw the hand-to-hand trade of drugs, fiends on queue to score. Under the streetlamp everything was done in a rush, only the hookers tread slowly. On one corner of the block, a man mercilessly stomped his wife, while undercover cops sat in unmarked cars scoping it all from the other end. Coco walked over to the kitchen table and sat counting the number of roaches darting across the wooden floor. The ringing telephone startled her. She recently had it reinstalled.

"Coco cannot speak with anyone right now... Yes, she'll be at school tomorrow. Who is this? Goodnight, Deedee." Coco bobbed her head to the beat on the radio. She watched her mother pacing back and forth through the kitchen. Sometimes it was to get a drink from the refrigerator, other times, like now, from the corner of her eyes she caught her staring.

"You're not gonna sit up in da kitchen waitin' for me to

fall asleep, Coco. You need to take your ass to bed right now," Mrs. Harvey said. "I'm a go to the corner store and you best have your ass up in that bed by time I get back."

"Mommy, are you sure? I'll go with you and..."

"Coco you must be suffering from short term memory cause you were there when your P O told you that you had a seven o' clock curfew. I don't need you out there, alright. I'm a grown woman and you're a child." Mrs. Harvey said as she slammed the door and locked it. Coco ran to the door.

Coco became concerned after a length of time had passed since her mother left. She walked to the kitchen window. She stood there and stared at the drug dealers on their grind right beneath her window. Her eyes searched, hoping to catch a glimpse of her mother. Eventually she returned to the living room, sat down on the sofa and stared at the clock.

Her mother later walked in the room followed by a sickly stench of burnt plastic, mingled with sweat. She immediately ran to the bathroom. After washing, she walked to the kitchen but like the tail on a skunk, the smell trailed her. She grabbed a bottle of beer with one hand and a cigarette in the other.

"You might as well move your bed this side o' the room," she said as perspiration poured profusely from her winded body.

"Ma, why are you sweating so hard? It ain't even that hot outside I mean..."

"Coco you need to handle your BI and lemme handle mine."

"Tell me why as soon as you come back, that smell is all

over the place? Tell me, mommy!" Coco ordered.

"First of all if you were implying that I was smokin' I had a talk with ah... that short black... ooh..."

"Rightchus," Coco offered closely taking aim at her mother's condition. "And he's number one crack-head..."

"Well I wasn't with him too long to find out if he's number one or two in the crack world. He wuz tellin' me 'bout how da cops did illegal search and all." Mrs. Harvey said while her hands moved all over her upper body, scratching.

"Stop it mommy, stop it!" Coco yelled.

"Coco dear, what's the matter with you?"

"Mommy your question should be 'what's the matter with us?'" Coco said and walked away.

She checked the door to make sure that the apartment was secure and searched her mother's wallet for her keys. Coco then turned off the light and sat by the door while her mother finished the beer.

"Coco lemme out so I can go get another beer," Mrs. Harvey pleaded.

"No way, mommy! You're not going out for the rest of the night. That's so not happening."

"So you're just gonna sit right there an' sleep. Didn't I tell you to go to sleep before I came back? All right stay there don't you move. Stay right there, Coco. You stubborn like your damn father."

She sat in the dark and after awhile drifted off to sleep. Coco was awaken by the buzzing of the doorbell. She looked over and saw that her mother was asleep. Coco walked to the window and raised it.

"Who da fuck is ringing my damn doorbell, let a nigga get some rest." Coco saw Rightchus emerging from the shadows. "Rightchus what da fuck is so important?"

"Why don't you ask your mother? She's da one paging me nine one, one."

"She's asleep alright. So get da fuck on, muthafucka!" Coco slammed the window. She stared at her mother grumbling something inaudible. Coco brought a blanket and placed it over her mother's outstretched figure. She fell asleep on the new sofa listening to her mother's relentless heavy snoring.

FOURTEEN

Next morning while waiting on the bus for school, Coco scanned the streets of her neighborhood looking for any sign of Rightchus. She had left her mother fast asleep. Coco suspected that it would only be a matter of time before her mother would be up and back on the streets searching for a high. Her only lookout, Miss Katie was in the hospital recovering from a stroke.

A bus pulled to a stop and she readied to board. She kept her eyes peeled for Rightchus as she stepped on. Coco found a seat and slipped away in her headphones tripping on her own voice spitting lyrics.

By the time she entered the school building, she realized that the news of her arrest had preceded her. Everywhere she went Coco heard the whispers behind arched eyebrows and saw fingers pointing. The tension was enough to initiate a nicotine crave. Coco searched her pockets then remembered she had left her cigarettes in the hood. Coco bopped to the corner store but when she tried to cop a loose one, the vendor gave her static.

"I've been copping loosies for years, yo. Habib, you know me, yo. I'm a senior at da school down the block..." Coco said. The store vendor did not budge.

"All you say is good. However, we are under strict order not to sell you any beers or cigarettes, Coco. You are a rapper. You are somebody famous. I did not know this. Even the police know you."

"What police? Who're you talking...?" Coco started to say but the store vendor quickly interrupted when other customers started to complain.

"Two DT's one black one white... that will be one dollar, sir... two detectives. If you're not getting anything else, you must leave the store. You cannot hang here!"

"Fuckin' Habib jerk! Damn, why didn't I remember to snatch madukes' cigarettes?" She was making her way back to school when Deedee ran toward her and hugged her.

"What's good, Dee?"

"Coco oh my God, Coco what's really good, girl. Coco you haven't called and..."

"Chill and I'll tell you all about it, yo. But before I do, you got stogies, yo?"

"Uh huh, here," Deedee offered Coco the pack.

Quickly she extracted one and immediately lit it. Her cheeks collapsed from the pulling action.

"Oh, you really needed that huh?"

"Word, in da worse way, yo. Shit was bananas I'm tellin' you, Dee." Coco announced. "Miss Katie is still in the hospital.

Dee, she had a stroke, yo."

"For real? How bad is she?"

"I don't know the details. But they doing all kinds of test and stuff."

"I'm sorry to hear about that, Coco..."

"My head is too tight for me to be up in class, but I know I gotta go. Dee, I can't be late. I'll tell you all about it later, ahight yo." Coco yelled as she disappeared inside the building.

Deedee stood with a quizzical look on her face. She glanced across the street and saw two pairs of eyes behind sunglasses peering at her. They were sitting in a black Caprice. She glanced back, and then made her way inside the school.

Throughout lunch, there was a closed meeting in the principal's office. Coco slouched in the chair staring in bewilderment at the principal. A Guidance counselor, teacher, and the vice-principal explained that the school board no longer considered Coco eligible for any scholarships.

"I think I've done well in this school. I'm always on the dean's list and all my grades are way above average, you said so yourselves." Coco responded.

"We agree Coco. But policy is policy and I'm afraid by you going and getting arrested you violated the strictest code of the school and therefore you're no longer eligible to participate in the scholarship program."

Coco skipped afternoon class and hung with a group of kids in the hallway until the end of the school day. Deedee encountered Coco leaving school after the last bell had sounded.

"Coco, Coco, wait up." Deedee yelled excitedly.

"Dee," Coco flashed the peace sign and walked over to Deedee.

"Where were you I was looking for you at lunch and..."

"I had to see that guidance counselor bitch, Martinez and the principal. It's all fucked up."

"You look like you could use a ride somewhere, Coco?"

"Yeah, that'll be cool if you can drop me home right quick. I wanna go to the hospital and see Miss Katie, but I gotta go home and look out for madukes first. She's up to..." Coco paused.

"Miss Katie is really bad huh?"

"Miss Katie," Coco started then paused. "I mean I really don't know, Dee. Shit's crazy... po-po came and bagged my ass. You gotta another stogie for me, yo?"

"Sure Coco," Deedee obliged. Both lit their cigarettes. "Why were you arrested for the shooting? It was that other girl who had a gun, I don't understand?"

"They say they found a bag a weed. Fucking Hip Hop police, they ain't nothing but two ol' lame ass dicks. They came at me cuz o' the shooting but they came on some next shit too, yo. Figure I'm gonna rat on somebody or sump'n. They got me in some type of probationary program, and gave me some mean-ass PO. Then when he tested me, of course it came back positive. I mean I can't even smoke no weed, yo. I'm stressed, I can't smoke weed and I can't drink. Things so fucked up, I can't even cop a stogie from da corner store. The Habib wasn't even trying to see my money, yo."

"Speaking of seeing you, those two officers from the investigation at my uncle's apartment were sitting out here today. I caught them watching us from their car."

"Say word? Why da fuck am I under this crazy surveillance, yo. I ain't no criminal. Shit's bananas!"

"They putting you through a lot, huh Coco? They got worse crimes going on out there and they picking on you. That is crazy."

"Tell me about it. They already spoke with Martinez and the principal. They asses be tellin' me I'm better off getting a GED or applying for job corps. Those haters actually told me it would be a waste of my time to even apply at a junior college. Are you fuckin' kidding me? I have to give up my education for a bag a weed? Give me a break." Coco said.

A black Mercedes came to a stop before them. The car joined traffic.

"One tenth and Lennox," Deedee said telling told the driver to take Coco home.

The Benz came to a stop outside her apartment and Coco was ready to get out.

"Coco if you want I'll get the driver to wait and then give you a ride to the hospital," Deedee suggested.

"That be cool, yo. I'll check upstairs and be right back," Coco said running from the vehicle.

A few minutes later, she returned with a cigarette dangling between her lips. Coco was about to get inside the car then abruptly changed her direction and quickly walked to the other side of the street. Deedee's eyes curiously followed Coco who was talking with Rightchus. Deedee let the window down in order to hear the conversation.

"Don't be selling her that shit. You hear me bum-ass

nigga, don't be seeing her. Or I'm a come see you and fuck your shit up..."

"Cuz you see me in da street doin' ma thing, don't mean you know me, ahight, Coco?"

"Rightchus, I'm telling you. You ain't shit but a crack-head."

"And I'm tellin' you just cuz you see shit this way don't necessarily mean they that way. I'm tellin' you if your mother wasn't a crack head you wouldn't be calling me one. I remember when your mother used to wake up crack head crabby, looking for me. She was soo skinny you could see her brain stems coming out da back of her head."

"Just remember nigga, I will come looking for your lil' ol' ugly ass..."

"I do you a favor, I'll tell you where them bitches, Kim and her girl, Tina hangout. Them is who you got beef wit' Coco, not me. I ain't busting no gun at you."

Coco shook her head and walked back to the car.

"Is everything alright, Coco?" Deedee asked.

"Yeah, yeah, it's all good. I just had to straighten out some shit wit that Shawty wop. Can I get a ride over to the hospital, yo?"

"How's your mom?"

"She wasn't even upstairs."

They reached the hospital a few minutes later. Deedee gave Coco a pack of cigarettes. Coco pocketed them.

Inside the hospital there were people scurrying back and forth. Impatient patients chasing exhausted doctors, hiding behind the nurses. She sought the information booth, gave Miss Katie's name and was directed to the eighth floor. Coco's palms sweated as she checked the name outside each opening in her effort to locate Miss Katie. A nurse caught Coco wandering.

"I'm tryin to find Miss Katie Patterson... ah... she's..."

"Patterson? Hmm I don't think she's able to have visitors yet. Are you a family member? We could make an exception, but I know she's still in intensive care..."

"Coco what's going on?"

Both Coco and the nurse turned and saw Rachel Harvey. The immediate smell of alcohol let Coco know that her mother had been drinking. Coco quickly tugged at her mother's arm and dragged her away.

"Thank you," she said to the nurse.

"Mommy you're such an embarrassment." Coco started to speak but went silent when she saw a group of doctors and nurses. They reached the elevator landing and waited.

"But Coco they had me waitin' what was I supposed to do?" Rachel Harvey said in hushed tones.

"Wait..."

"It made me a lil' unbalance when they told me that Miss Katie might not make it. Coco, I couldn't take it. I had to go and get a lil' nip of sump'n... that's all."

"Shush, ahight... what d'ya mean Miss Katie may not make it?"

"When I got here it was about one o' clock and I had a chance to conversate with the doctors an' all..."

"And what?" Coco asked when an elevator came and her mother stepped inside. "This one's going up. We're waiting to go down."

"What goes up must come down," Rachel Harvey said. Most of the other riders laughed.

FIFTEEN

It was much later when Coco reached her block. She immediately spotted her mother parlaying with street hustlers of the hood. The crowd was about a stone's throw away from the corner store. It was the crack spot. Rightchus was in the center of the mix. Coco boldly walked over to the abandoned building where they were scrambling and yanked on her mother's arm.

"What da hell..." Rachel Harvey spun around still furiously sucking on the glass stem. Beads of sweat formed on her forehead. The veins in her face protruded as if someone had a vice grip on her neck, choking her, cutting her circulation. Her eyes rolled back in her head when she realized it was her daughter. Coco smacked the pipe from her mother's ashy lips and hauled her away from the group.

She led her mother across the street and away from the disciples of crack. They entered the building and got on the elevator.

"Ya gotta enjoy life before you go six foot under. Life's

short 'fore you know it, you da next one dead," Rachel Harvey drawled.

Coco looked at her mother's face, which was completely powdered from by her high. They got off the elevator and Coco half carried, her half dragged her, through the door and into the apartment.

"Mom, is it fear that makes you go get high?"

"Coco," she slurred. "I don't get high, girl. That's your thing."

"So what d'ya call what you were doin' just now?"

"I was only buggin' with Rightchus an' them. They the ones gettin' all high an shit. They droppin' purple pills, blue ones and all kind a shit..."

"And poor ol' you weren't doin' anything right, ma?"

"I wuz lookin' out, you know Rightchus, he big timin' an' such. He got a lot of connections and his connections gave him much, much crack... real good stock too..."

"Ma, I'm warning you, you better stay away from that damn crack head cuz he's gonna take all your money."

Her mother chuckled.

"Yes, house warden. I'm alright. No need for you to get yourself all excited..." Rachel offered and closed her eyes. Coco sat next to her and clicked on the television. Rachel Harvey watched and laughed for a moment. Before long, her mother was snoring. Later Coco heard her mother rise and in zombie-like fashion roamed the apartment, going from room to room. Coco kept a keen eye as her mother drank glass after glass of water. Mrs. Harvey's journey ended in the bathroom.

"Ma, you okay in there, yo?"

"Coco what did I tell you about using 'yo'- when you conversatin' wit me? Ain't you supposed to be asleep already? It's way pass your bedtime."

"I'm staying up to keep you company."

"Don't do me any favors. Now take your ass to sleep. You know you gotta go to school early in the morning."

SIXTEEN

Eric Ascot sat in a booth with Maruichi and his sons. They were sipping champagne and laughing up a storm. Maruichi was in his stylish couture dapper and played with a huge diamond on his right pinky. Eric mentioned the idea of a beautiful vacation and Maruichi unveiled his lethal charm.

"Don't think I don't understand your dilemma Eric, fugheddabout it. A woman wants to be pleased and I think taking her to San Tropez will be great for the both of you. Here's to great living," Maruichi said and raised his glass. The others at the table did likewise.

"May I suggest also that the south of Italy very romantic and there are some great resorts there..." Maruichi said kissing his own fingers.

Eric handed over a roll of twenty thousand dollars. Maruichi's sons counted it.

"Shame on you guys." Maruichi said with a slap to his son's hand. "I'm sorry Eric but I'm afraid my boys are raised by myself. I have always taught them not to trust anyone. This a mere formality but it's all worthwhile. Ah... my security boys that went with your niece reported there was a minor problem. Apparently, on Sunday evening a fight broke out in this Harlem apartment complex where a friend of your niece resides."

"A fight? My niece was involved in a fight in Harlem. That's crazy. What happened?"

"Well not much but a friend of your niece was fighting. We were able to squash it. But you know, that kind of protection we offer to rap groups because of gunplay, there are usually extra charges. This one we handled for you. Eric you understand don't you? If this type of scenario happens again it gets added as business charges. I can't control that, only you can."

"You sure it was Sunday huh? Friends of my niece were fighting, huh?" Eric asked in disbelief. "And Dee was there? She didn't..." Eric started and let his voice trailed off

"You met my girl? Of course you have," Maruichi said Eric nodded.

"Maybe, I might have..."

"Anyway she's got these ah... plans to become another MTV superstar..."

"And you want me to...?"

"If you could, please it would be a tremendous favor. Maybe we could talk about excusing tributes in exchange for a record deal. If you get a chance, think about it. Let me know, in a day or so," Maruichi said and sipped.

"Hey dad, did you mention yet how them fucking cops trying to get that no good bastard out?"

"Yeah, Johnny here made some news. He found out that our man wants to sing for the government in order to be sprung from the can. The fucking bastard got some nerves, uh? Fugeddaboutit. We got our people to handle that thing with kids' gloves. You follow me, Eric? That should be of no concern of yours, you got me?" Maruichi leaned over and patted Eric's shoulder.

"Excuse me a second," he said and walked away from the booth. Eric walked to the bar and dialed from his cell phone. He listened to the ring then after the outgoing message played, he spoke. "Soph, give me a call please." He closed the phone and walked back to the booth where Maruichi was holding court.

"Oh Eric I was just telling the boys here, how important it is to have right people around you and that applies to marriage, even..."

"Absolutely," Eric nodded approvingly. He saw another bottle of expensive champagne on the table. Knowing it was already on his tab, Eric poured another glass of the bubbly.

"Me, I believe in the law of omerti," Maruichi said while sipping.

"What exactly is that?" Eric asked.

"It's a code of silence established way back in da early times in Sicily," Maruichi answered drinking the last of bubbly in the glass. "Here stateside, I'm afraid not too many people honor the code. Everybody from your wife, the mistress, friends, they all wanna belong to a choir. No honor..."

Eric wandered out the bar and into a waiting limo.

"Where to boss?" The chauffer asked.

"Drop me at the studio B. I've got some work to do." Eric calmly said.

It was late and her eyes burned from the strain of a tense day, Sophia checked the message and decided to return Eric's call right away. She did not want him to know that she had been dodging him. All he does is stay in the studio, she thought as she dialed his number.

"I'm returning your call," she said desperately holding down the thrill she felt after hearing his voice. "Eric, what is it? What's wrong? I've been working all day, but I'm all ears... I'm here," she said after awhile. I can't give you a complete answer right now. Maybe I'll have to work or you know... I've got couple trials that I've got to prep for and... Not that it'll cost me my job. It's, it's just that... I'll call and let you know, all right Eric. I must get some rest, so goodnight, Eric. I'll call and confirm, all right."

Eyes closed, yet wide awake while resting on her back, Sophia kept on asking herself repeatedly: 'Why did I answer his call?' The answer never materialized and the question nagged and kept her up most of the night. She analyzed her situation and made the call at about three in the morning. By then there was no one else in the studio but Eric. Sophia knew that he relished working on his music alone. The phone rang once then twice.

"Eric, Eric," she said hurriedly afraid to be stopped. "I'll

meet with you over the weekend," she hung up without waiting for an answer.

SEVENTEEN

Next morning, school was not the same for Coco. She did not show-up for any of her classes. She hung in the hallway smoking. A the end of the day, she spotted Deedee waiting outside school.

"What's poppin' Dee?" She asked greeting the girl.

"Coco I haven't seen you all day. What's up?" Deedee queried and gave Coco a hug. "You don't like your classes anymore, girl?"

"Yeah, I still like learning and shit. But..."

"But what, Coco? You used to be all about school and then all of a sudden you're not attending classes. You're busy letting what some folks say affect yor behavior, you've gotta be you..."

The blast from a Benz's horn interrupted Deedee. She turned and saw the driver signaling her. "Coco, do you want a ride? Take us to one tenth and Lenox and then to the hospital." Deedee requested. The chauffer waved his index finger several times.

"No can do, Miss."

"What're you talking about? You did yesterday?"

"Yeah, but this is today and I got orders from the boss."

"What boss? Who's your boss?"

"You can call your Uncle alright. I told you we're not going there..."

"Dee, it's cool girlfriend. I got a bus pass, yo. I'll use it, ahight?"

"Are you sure, Coco? I mean I could call my uncle and clean up this mess..."

"Nah ain't no use for all the dramas. I'm good. I'll hop on da bus. See you again, Dee."

Coco lit a cigarette, waved and was in her bop as she made her way to the bus stop. Coco threw the cigarette away and hopped aboard when the bus arrived. She quickly found a seat and fixed her headphones in place.

She arrived at the hospital and saw her mother waiting with flowers.

"Ma, is everything okay?" She asked and stopped in front of her mother, eagerly she awaited an answer.

Mrs. Harvey peered from beneath tired lids.

"Coco, why you just be bum rushing all the time? What da hell's wrong wit 'cha? You could scare the shit out of somebody. One o' these days you gonna get it runnin' up on me like that..."

"I saw you sitting here and..."

"And what, girl? This where you s'pose to sit till they let you upstairs. That's why it sez 'waitin area' out front. You can read can't you? Speakin' of readin', got a letter from da school today. Why you ain't say nuthin' bout them bootin' you out da scholarship program, Coco?"

"Huh, ah... I was gonna mention but..."

"But you wanted to hide it from me. Things you try to hide is comin' to light, Coco," Rachel Harvey said while staring down her daughter.

"First of all lemme drop this on ya, can't nobody put a limit to the knowledge you can attain. If you want it, you can get it. That's the American way. But by you not goin' to all these classes, you doin' them a huge favor. That's what they want you to do. They want you to give up, to surrender. Then they beat you Coco. You'll be the loser without a high school degree. Ha, I even got mine..." Mrs. Harvey said looking at her daughter.

"Not when I gotta worry that you gonna be goin' an' doin' all tha..."

"Watch your mouth 'fore I split it open. You need to worry about Coco and stop sweatin' urrh-one else." Rachel Harvey said.

"You may go and visit the patient. Visiting hours started," the hospital police announced. Coco signed in and rode the elevator in silence with her mother standing close by. They were shown to the room and both went inside. There was a nurse leaving.

"You can only see her for a few minutes. I'll take the flowers. She may or may not respond. She will be able to sense your presence."

"How long before she can go..."

"Go home? Hmm, it may not be for a while. She's had a stroke and a heart attack. The result is a coma. Although she's more stable, she still has a long way to go, sweetheart. You can speak to her and maybe she may or may not respond." The nurse took the flowers and placed them in a vase with the others.

Coco felt sadness as she sat next to the bed and watched the respirator system moving up and down.

"They got her on life support," Rachel Harvey said with tears streaming down her eyes. "Oh God bless you Miss Katie." She said and fidgeted with her handbag. After a couple minutes of uneasiness, she addressed Coco. "I can't stand all this. I'll be downstairs in the waiting area when you're done. I just cannot stand to see this poor lady hooked up to all this machinery."

"Hi Miss Katie, I know you can hear me. This Coco, since you got your eyes shut. I miss you. I'm so sorry I got into that fight. Those girls they been tryin' to jump me every time they see me. And it led to all this. I was arrested Miss Katie. They claim I know shi... I mean info on police murder and all this sh... ah... stuff." Coco stood in shock when an alarm sounded. Couple of nurses came charging into the room. She watched in horror as they checked Miss Katie.

"I'm afraid you'll have to leave..." One of them said. Coco backed out slowly as they drew the curtain around Miss Katie. With tears in her eyes, Coco left the room and headed for the elevator.

EIGHTEEN

Eric was working in his usual electronic trance. Lately all the head honchos of every major label were in touch with him. These opportunities only came knocking so often. He divided his day so that he could spend time working on his music. Eric sat at the controls fidgeting with backing tracks. He adjusted the volume when he heard the phone ringing.

"What's going on, Dee?"

"Uncle, Uncle E., I've been trying to reach you all evening."

"What's the matter, Dee?"

"Uncle, why did the driver refuse to take Coco home? She doesn't live far from the school. It wasn't like it was that far, uncle. I mean, they all lazy and you paying them and they come off like they the boss..."

"Well, I told him not to. See, whenever Coco is around, bullets flying and you gotta break out the bulletproof vest..."

"But Uncle..."

"Dee, why didn't you tell me about the fight on Sunday?"

"But it wasn't Coco's fault these girls..."

"It doesn't matter whose fault it is Dee, I don't want you around violence all day. I mean, you've got to be careful and I just don't wanna lose you. That would kill me, you understand?"

"Yes, Uncle E., I understand."

"But for now, do me a favor and just stay away from Coco and her problems."

"But she's my friend..."

"Ain't nothing wrong with talking with her on the telephone and you see her at school, but as far as hanging-out with her, leave all of that out, at least for now, okay."

"All right, but uncle when the cops..."

"Dee, that doesn't require any further discussion."

Eric ended the call and sat back listening to the same track. The phone rang again. Shaking his head, Eric stared at the phone a beat before picking it up.

"Yeah, Dee, go ahead," he said.

"Whassup muthafucka?"

"Who this?"

"This me bitch ass. Your worse muthafucking nightmare. What's up?" Lil' Long responded. Eric began to record the call. "I'm coming for ya. Go ahead and report this to the DA pussy ass nigga and I got some extra slugs for your fat ass. Fuck you!"

The call ended abruptly and Eric checked the security monitors. He walked out the studio and got a cigarette. Eric reflected, took a drag then dialed Maruichi.

NINETEEN

Dusk fell when Coco and her mother made their way back to the neighborhood. A short, dark skinned man wearing a black turban was attracting a small crowd.

"There goes that nigga Rightchus, always using some kind of happening to make his cheddar. That lil' nigga is king crack head he stays busy, yo," Coco said.

"... This is just another sign o' the times. Give to the Rightchus brothers and sisters the end is on us..."

"People are actually reaching for their wallets," Coco noted.

"He be doin' his damn thing. Can't knock his hustle," Mrs. Harvey said reflectively.

"You'd never know," Coco said with an irritated tone.

Coco stared in the direction of the crowd as she spoke.

"We all wanna get da hell outta this damn hole. Coco I know you do but just buying nice furniture ain't gonna change what it is," Mrs. Harvey said as she walked through the door. "Coco I know you's upset about school an' all but we can rise above this."

"But everything seems to go against me. I mean school..."

"Tell you what I'm gonna have a meeting with them damn school board people an' I'm just gonna give 'em a piece of my mind. I mean the nerve, they can't tell you no when you're not doin' time. You're not a criminal an' they cannot kick you out of the scholarship program. I called the channcelor's office and they looking into it.

"Really, you did, mom?"

"I did. Coco, girl madukes a fighter and that's why you gotta keep on trying. You know life ain't easy when you from the ghetto. I know it's my fault with all my ways and your father not being around, but I don't want you to grow up and be like me, Coco. I don't want you to make what anyone do, cause you to give up on your dreams."

"I'm not gonna lose, ma. But I can't win without your help."

"That's my baby talkin'." Mrs. Harvey said.

"Ma, you know I gotta concentrate an' I mean, you can't go wandering off doin' your thing. This gonna take teamwork and I'm expecting you to handle your part," Coco said and searched her mother's eyes. The doorbell rang.

"Herb Ward, here to see you, ah Mrs. Harvey."

"Okay, come on up." Rachel Harvey replied.

Coco looked at the time. Couple minutes after eight. Ward walked into the apartment and spoke privately with Mrs.

Harvey for a short time before turning his attention to Coco.

"How's everything going, Coco?"

"I'm alright."

"You getting kicked out of the scholarship program have anything to do with why you're not attending your classes?" Ward asked and waited a beat for an answer.

"Coco, open your mouth and speak up, the man is asking you a question." Mrs. Harvey said.

"I thought I answered it already."

"Mrs. Harvey thank you, but I'll handle this, please. Coco, why aren't you going to your classes?"

"I just did not feel like going to school period, but I know I need something that sez 'I can read'. So I'll stay in school, ahight?"

"Coco wha' I tell you 'bout that street talk shit?"

"Well, Coco that seems to be what we all want. If there're any problems before Tuesday, please feel free to call me at the office, okay Coco. I don't want to hear any reports of you missing school."

Coco closed her eyes as the door slammed when she was assured that Ward had left. She went to the kitchen with pen and pad. Coco slipped her headphones around her ears and began writing. It was an uphill battle from day to day, but she was confident that she could accomplish her goals and her mother would have to do the same.

Later that same evening, detectives found Rightchus lounging on the corner eyeing the scene. He would be the perfect pitch man. Hall calculated. Kowalski got out the car with Hall closely behind him and Rightchus started backpedaling when he noticed the detectives walking toward him.

"Rightchus, come here. Didn't I tell you to go get a job? What are you still doing here on the corner? Come talk to me," Hall shouted as he approached Rightchus, who immediately took off running. Kowalski and Hall were in hot pursuit. A few blocks away they caught up to him and dragged him into a building.

"Now don't have us chasing you all over the place. Matter fact, you're going downtown with us," Hall announced for all gathered to hear. Kowalski went for the car while Hall frisked Rightchus.

"Got anything on you that's gonna..." Hall started to ask but Rightchus cut him off.

"An' if I say I do, is you gonna not search a brotha?" Rightchus asked irritated by the treatment. "Y'all better not try anything cuz I know my rights. I'm innocent until you prove me guilty."

TWENTY

The annoying ring of the doorbell announced Tina. Kimberly could hear the chimes from twenty feet away in the bathroom of her two-bedroom apartment.

"I'll be right there, bitch," she said continuing to give her son, Roshawn a bath.

The doorbell rang incessantly.

"I said I'm coming. Wait a minute, bitch."

Kimberly opened the door.

"Got to go potty," Tina said and hurried to the bathroom.

"Roshawn, you wanna watch TV, while mommy talk to Aunt Tina? She's loca, son. What's up? Why yo gotta to be rushing up in here and blowing up my bathroom?"

"Aunt Tina is very pretty," Tina said to Roshawn. She jumped in his face and playfully planted a kiss on his cherub cheek. The boy let go with a gleeful and joyous chuckle.

Kimberly joined Tina already sitting at the kitchen table. She gazed at *Friends* on the muted television set.

"Getting to serious matters, guess who's coming home today?" Tina asked. The smile enveloped her face and enhanced her dimpled look. Her light brown eyes danced.

"That no-good, nickel and dime, drug-dealing-on-the-corner-cute-baby-daddy?"

"Yeah, girl. That's the one. Nesto's coming home. You think I'm happy or what?" A jubilant Tina asked.

"All I'm saying is girlfriend don't make it too much harder on you. Use protection. I know y'all gonna be fucking like rabbits. And the moment these broke ass niggas leave jail, they wanna come and stay with you, like they at some damn hotel. They don't want to go get a decent job or contribute to the household. But they wanna get mad and throw blows when you don't cook, clean and sex their ass off. Like the coochie is part of the release program. My PO sez, 'I'm released to your care'. My God. Let the nigga know you too can do bad by your lonesome. I used to tell Deja, God Bless his soul. I used to tell his no good ass not to try that shit. It's the same thing Mr. Nesto gonna be tryin'."

"Kim, you ain't even giving the nigga a chance, damn." Tina walked to the window.

"I did. I'm tired of seeing him use you like his damn floor mat whenever he wants to. You're the mother of his son. When was the last time his drug-dealing ass bought you or Junior, sump'n, huh?"

"You right, you right..."

"Anything for that matter? Answer that. When was the

last time?" Kimberly asked.

The doorbell sounded followed by impatent knocking. Tina went to check.

"Who's that banging on my door?" Kim asked.

"It's them DT's. The white boy told me we could make a deal and help them out. I was thinking that the other one might be your type. He's tall, black and good looking." Tina answered peering through the peephole.

"Bitch stop runnin' your trap and let the dicks in. Fool, you told them you be here or sump'n?" Kim asked and hurried to her son.

"Roshawn it's a good thing mommy wasn't smokin' any weed, cuz this fool done call the police on us. Don't be scared baby boy. The men won't bite you." Kimberly continued as Tina opened the door and both Kowalski and Hall walked inside.

"Good evening ladies," they both said. Tina bowed and smiled.

"I'm sure it will be." Tina said winking.

"You got that right, baby. Look at that, we're already hitting it off just right." Kowalski answered returning the wink.

TWENTY-ONE

Sophia Lawrence sat in a restaurant amongst a loud lunch hour rush crowd. She shared Club sandwiches and Penta water with Michael Johnson. He had asked her to meet him when she told him she was unavailable this weekend.

"You seem so pensive, what's the matter?" He asked after studying her profile.

"Can I be honest with you?" Sophia said glancing around.

"You better not try it..." Michael started to joke.

"No, Michael I'm serious," Sophia said sternly.

"Okay, go ahead, be honest..."

"I don't know a damn about anything that's going on in my life. Your office is considering an indictment against Eric for solicitation of murder charges. He could go to jail for life and I don't even know his role in all this."

"Look, I've been honest with you since I've known you,

and I have known you since..."

"Since law school, Michael I know, I know. It doesn't help me none to know the man I was about to marry is totally not who I've known him to be.

"I'm also looking for help."

"You cannot expect me to testify against Eric?"

"You may not have a choice. We... ah... the District attorney office will subpoena you."

"C'mon Michael you can tell them to put that in the shredder. You for one know, I know whole lot less than you do, what will I say? What can I do?"

"C'mon let's leave," Michael said assisting Sophia with her coat. He snapped a small button like object on the inside as he did so, then Michael quickly slipped a coin-sized transmitter into her Hermes Croc handbag, before handing it to her. They walked out into a slight drizzle of rain. Sophia pulled her coat tightly about her.

A black Crown Victoria pulled to a stop in front of them. Michael opened the door and Sophia got in.

"Sophia this is my partner in crime, Juan Rodriguez. Juan's a seasoned vet. He's been in office way before prohibition was passed." They both laughed while Sophia looked out the window. They dropped her off at her office building.

"Everything is set?"

"She's armed and ready," Michael said to Juan as they drove off.

"Good, then let's hope they have a great weekend," Juan said driving away. Michael plugged his head set in.

"Yeah it's working just fine. I can hear her calling him."

"Don't tell me you're going to be sitting here monitoring her every conversation are you?"

"It should be a rather interesting weekend for us." Michael said as the car settled into traffic.

"Yes, this is the closest we've been to shutting Maruichi down." Juan opined.

TWENTY-TWO

Sophia stood outside and waited a couple of minutes before she saw his Mercedes. The chauffer-driven vehicle came to a stop next to her. She stood in place until a rear window came down and Eric's voice bellowed at her.

"Sophia, Sophia over here," he said admiring her legs.

She walked over to the car and peeked in. "Hmm, you're full of surprises, aren't you?"

"I'm just trying to make things easier," Eric said.

"I've got to stop by and get some clothes and other stuff..."

"Ah... fuhgeddaboutit, let's just go. We have reservations for dinner at NY Nobu in about half hour. We'll pick up anything you need to get later."

Sophia liked that about Eric; right or wrong, he always took charge. Sophia sat back, relaxed and tried to enjoy the ride. Eric touched Sophia's arm. He searched her features looking for consent. He tenderly placed his lips on hers.

"Eric, no stop," she moaned.

He pulled away. A few minutes later, they were inside the restaurant.

The place was bustling with the jet-setting crowd. Eric and Sophia were quickly ushered to their waiting table.

Later when they were about to leave she saw Eric waving to someone. She recognized the mobster, Maruichi.

"Do you know anyone decent anymore? Or are all your friends gangsters?" She couldn't resist the quip.

"I know some decent folks, like you," Eric said grabbing her close.

"All right big Max we're going to the east Hamptons."

"Gotcha," was the response and the car took off in the night.

"We're here," Eric announced when they reached their destination. He stepped outside and held Sophia's arm as he guided her inside.

The tingling touch of soft lips against the back of his neck interrupted his stroll. Moist, gentle kisses caressed the week's stubbles of Ascot's cheek.

"You got to get a shave," she said.

"You're absolutely right," he agreed and bit her lips as he kissed her.

Her arms hugged him and Eric knew he had made the right choice. Eric hoisted her shapely body while Sophia was deep in his embrace. He lost control when Sophia returned his kiss. Sophia let out a sexy howl when Eric scooped and carried her slender, supple, honey-caramel frame straight to the bedroom at the top of the stairs. Her fingers were busy playing with his beard. The tip of her tongue stroked the length of his neck up and down.

She fell against Eric's chest and nibbled his exposed nipples. Her tongue made a circling motion, starting outside and moving in on the areola. She reached down and worked her hand to the area of his crotch. Her fingers encircled the entire package. Her fingers weighed one family jewel at a time then raked her nails over the sensitive skin.

Eric laid her on the bed and dove in after her. His ample girth getting the best of her lean loins. Their motion rocked the frame of the king-sized waterbed. Sophia stroked his shaft up and down until Eric was steaming from the sensation. He sprang up and tore the red Cosabella thongs from Sophia's shapely ass.

She quickly rolled over and Eric licked his fingers before he smacked her exposed cheeks in rapid succession. The stinging sensation drove her wild. Sophia grabbed his manhood and squeezed the love muscle.

"Hey baby, be easy with it," Eric panted. "I wanna make love, not start a war. All right?"

Her fingers stroked the shaft of his penis as the head disappeared into her mouth. She removed it from her mouth and stroked it gently against her breast. She rubbed the glowing tip against her opened moist lips letting the head to slip in and out. She opened her lips stroking the head between them until Eric was almost completely blissed out.

Sophia licked her fingers and slid her hand down to her shaven mound. With her eyes closed, she kneaded the area gently as her body swayed from side to side.

Eric eased her hot body onto the bed. Sophia moaned as she felt his hands slowly spreading her legs apart. She fondled her tits and moaned as Eric's lips made contact with her vagina. His tongue sought her clitoris. Sophia's body thrashed about uncontrollably.

He watched Sophia's performance with intense interest. His heartbeat increased violently with each pulse. He was ready to blow a valve. He could not hold back any longer. With lust, Eric sprang into action and curtailed Sophia's sexual dance with a thrust of his pulsating penis. Eric eased back and forth into her soft, wet, moistness. His down stroke eagerly greeted by Sophia's grinding hips. Every movement of her body was on point with the rhythm of his thrusting. A hiss of soft sounds escaped Sophia's throat. She arched her long, shapely legs about his waist. She reached up, nibbled his ear and bit his neck. Her teeth sank deep into his flesh. She edged closer to orgasmic bliss. "Yes, baby. Oh yes baby." Enraptured by the moment, her crescendo grew closer. Sophia crooned with her eyes tightly closed while her arms guided Eric's torso. Her legs now wrapped around his neck.

They stayed this way, him stroking harder and faster until Eric's panting came thick as if he was having a spasm. She watched carefully. Sophia could tell that the end was near by the way his nostrils flared. Eric was heaving even harder. She could feel the explosion gripping his body.

Sophia quickly dislodged his throbbing shaft. She was just in time for creamy fluid to be ejaculated all over her face. Fluid continued to drip from Eric's penis. Sophia ground her moistness up and down on his torso. She then slipped her mouth over his dick and tortuously slow, licked from the base to the tip of the shaft.

She sucked him back to life. Eric felt her hot moistness when Sophia straddled his erection. Slowly she began to ride up and down. He reached up and caressed her ass cheeks then his digit slipped into her brown hole. Her hips moved faster and faster. Sophia grabbed her hair, grinding her body until her neck snapped back and she moaned loudly.

Sophia was doubled over and bucking. She was ready and her ass waved with wild abandon. She reached between her legs and naughtily kneaded his love package. Eric grunted and felt his motion automatically increased. Sophia wiggled her hips and shook her ass, real fast. All the time she jiggled his balls with her hand underneath her crotch. Eric tried to keep up but eventually gave up and enjoyed the ride.

"Yeah, baby my baby my sweets. Ah yes I love you," he yelled as he felt the build up in his stomach. His lips went dry and sweat came profusely. "Oh-h ah-h yes baby here it comes-s-s-s..." Eric erupted like a broken dam and Sophia continued to let her hips and ass do the riding, her desire still ablaze.

TWENTY-THREE

Cloaked in a white terry cloth robe and Sean Jean blue boxers, Eric Ascot dragged his Hermes sandals to the front lawn. He pulled out a mini recording device and mumbled into it, turned it off and returned it to his pocket. He was always ready for a new din.

He glanced at the newspaper in his hand. He saw 'headline investigation concerning dirty cops.' The next page contained a picture of himself, Sophia, and Maruichi taken last night at the restaurant. The caption read, "cozying up to mob boss." It mentioned he and Maruichi by name. Sophia was just in the picture.

Sophia joined Eric on the lawn. He quickly folded the newspaper and tucked it under his arm.

"How'd you like this to go on for about a week or so?" he asked leading her back to the house.

"A week or so, don't tempt me Eric, you know I could use a vacation, baby." Sophia placed wet kisses on his neck.

"Let's take one," Eric said.

"Eric I haven't had a real one in a long time."

"So, let's start planning something, somewhere, maybe San Tropez..."

Sophia's eyes sparkled when she looked at him. She kissed him and walked away. The legal eagle went straight to her laptop and logged on to the web. Before long she was sighing at the tourists' attractions.

"I need a few winks," Eric said as she walked into the house heading toward his bedroom.

"All right big man, but you can't sleep all day. We've got to book our flight to San Tropez," Sophia sang while grabbing the newspaper.

Hours later, when he finally awoke Eric was greeted by an evil glare from Sophia. Despite her obvious anger, Sophia looked resplendent in her Channel skirt suit.

"What's the matter, hon?"

"You didn't want me to read about you being a damn mafia earner and all the other names they were calling you. You have some nerves, Eric sweet-talking me to go on a vacation with you," Sophia said accusingly. "What you were planning, have me on the lam, running from the law? Cause that's who will be coming after you, Eric. Why can't you be honest with me?"

"There's nothing honest about that. The article dealt with two bad cops who got killed. In fact it referred to them as rogue cops. Whoever took the picture was only trying to link me with Maruichi by saying what? I'm part of their organization. I'm not a member of the mob. You know you can't believe anything in the news. You know those people only give partial truth." Eric looked serious and concerned.

"Eric this is very serious. Can you please tell me why you're under investigation."

"I make good music and they have to know where all the deadly sound coming from." He responded lightheartedly. His fear and his need showed plainly through his attempt at an awful joke. He watched Sophia sadly shaking her head.

"I don't understand that if you love me, why can't you just trust me and tell me what's really going on, Eric?" She asked sobbing.

"This shit all started when I ah... well you know how close me and Busta was? Before he got killed we had ah... taken out this contract for the ones who raped Deedee. I told him about the rape and he was mad. He's Deedee's godfather. Then bullets started flying. Before you know it, he's dead and the cops..."

"Eric wouldn't it have been better cooperating with the police in the first place?"

"Yeah, maybe, I mean in retrospect I should've, but what's done is done," Eric said in a flat, bored voice.

"Why didn't it stop there? Why was there bloodshed? There are men chasing you..."

"Maybe it's connected, maybe it's not. Like I said, I really don't know the details of what Busta did. I know the first one turned out to be the wrong guy and eventually we got the right guy."

"I don't want to hear anymore. Eric, you could go to jail for life. Conspiracy to commit murder, solicitation to commit murder, and at least about two counts of murder, oh my God! How could you Eric? Now you've aligned yourself to... Ah these people with mobster connections and you actually think things are going to be easier? I'm an attorney. How do you think this makes me look? I could get disbarred." Sophia angrily stated.

"That's it," Eric said in the flat voice of defeat.

"I don't want to hear from you until you resolve this Eric. You cannot be serious about getting married under these conditions. Call the car, Eric I've had enough."

TWENTY-FOUR

It had been three weeks since Lil' Long had been hauled into solitary confinement. The place was dark and it stunk. He smelled himself and felt sick. Blood had leaked from his stomach and was caked on his belly. His thoughts were churning when he heard the metallic scraping of the early warning system.

CO's on the floor. The light struck Lil' Long's eyes forcing him to shield them.

"All right, come with us," a guard said. They hosed Lil' Long down in the shower. From there they issued a change of clothes and escorted him to the infirmary. "Oh I'm so sorry you got caught by those rat hunters. It's amazing how word gets around real fast, huh?" Igor stopped by to see Lil' Long.

"Look man, I don't care about anything. I want out of here, today if possible."

"That's good it must mean that you are prepared to cooperate with us?"

"Yeah, man you da muthafuckin' boss," Lil' Long answered.

"We'll make the arrangements. But first there's the matter of a certain chess championship that must be returned as part of the tribute..."

"Say no mo', man. Just tell me when and I'll take the dive."

"We'll arrange it for next week. Shortly after that, you'll be free to go. We'll have a job for you."

"Ahight, man, whateva you say."

The most fragile weapon in a mobster's arsenal is his ego. Lil' Long appeased Igor's in a return chess match, where he allowed the Russian to win not just once but even in the rematch.

Six weeks after going inside, Lil' Long was released and slipped back easily into the community. The first thing was to get money. Lil' long stayed in and slept all day playing with his toys: Play station, and his guns of choice, twin Desert Eagles. He cocked and un-cocked the weapons numerous times, aiming and dreaming of the moment. Other times he would slip out to the corner store, disguising himself in wig and make-up. He read the newspaper and followed the news of Eric Ascot's connection. He can be touched, Lil' Long thought as he stared at pictures in the newspaper.

Six O' clock the next morning, Lil' Long heard the loud banging on his door. Grabbing his guns he was about to jet.

"Open up!"

He heard and then the sound of the door coming off the hinges and falling on him. Lil' Long was knocked out. Later, he awoke in an office with no windows. He was shackled to an iron desk and chair in a corner. A putrid odor emanated from the area.

Lil' Long sat on the floor of the city parole office. His gut was aflame with the pain of being repeatedly hit with the flashlight of a disgruntled parole officer. He ran his hand over the stitches in his stomach. He gritted his teeth trying to hold back the urge to scream.

"See what you done cause? Ripped ma goddamn shirt, you son of a," Ward started.

"Easy, easy remember you're representing the system, I–"

"Shuddafuckup you bastard! Before I seriously violate your ass!"

"See there you go wid your cheap threats. I ain't goin' nowhere. I'm a be here when you retire, nah mean?" Lil' Long's face carried a smirk.

"Keep talking that yang and I'll send your crippled ass straight upstate, right now. I know some people who would be very happy to welcome a crippled bastard like you back into penal confinement. Ya heard me, maggot. They would like nothing better than to welcome you back to the joint," the angered parole officer said grabbing his crotch.

"For what though? What you gon' violate me for? I ain't done nothing wrong. So, whatever man. It's not like they let me out and... I... I... I be out there wilding and all. I'm saying, listen, ask the big cat. I'm not doing nothing. Just cooling, holding shit down and all." Lil' Long gazed up and realized the parole officer was in his face.

"One of my orders states that you must report your tired, crippled ass up in here every Thursday to my office for your drug testing. Now, when you come to see me, if I want to rip another asshole in you, then I do. You understand me scumbag?"

Lil' Long refused to acknowledge the question. It was then the parole officer grabbed him by the collar and asked the question again, this time he counted the words, the way mothers do when scolding a child.

"Do we understand each other?"

Lil' Long waited a little too long. The parole officer's breath was hot in his face. "I say, do you understand?"

Lil' Long tried to turn his head but the grip tightened, he felt like choking and the words came tumbling out.

"Y-y-e-e-ah man, I hear you. N-n-now c-c-can you get up off m-m-ma muthafuckin' neck," Lil' Long said with a stutter. The parole officer slowly released Lil' Long's neck and shoved him back into the chair.

"No exceptions. Now I don't give a damn who you know, or who knows you. You're mine. You follow my orders to the letter. Now, if I have to drive out to the hood and get you when you are supposed to be here, your ass is grass. Cause as far as I'm concerned, you ain't nothing but a fuck-up. Screw up. I will violate you."

The parole officer was standing over Lil' Long and pointing his finger.

Six months ago, everything was different. Lil' Long held the key to the gangster's empire. He knew respect brought in a lot of money, and he had the always livelier, Vulcha. He had juice and props. He was the man. Then Vulcha was gunned down in an ambush. Now, he was being hauled around like a common parolee, a sack of garbage. Now everyone spat on him.

"I still got it. I just need a couple of months to do my thing, heal up proper you know?" Lil' Long words came in almost a whisper.

"Huh?" answered the parole officer with a puzzled look.

"I'm saying, look at me, I still got it. Things ain't really the same but I can make it that way again. I'm saying nothing's change 'cept the way I fucking walk. I still got a chance to rep..."

"That's what you think. Here's the facts. You ain't got a chance to do nothing. The medical people, they don't have no faith in you, boy. They don't even think you'll ever regain your coordination. Your partner in crime is deep-six. You got no future as a gangster. I'll be right here to make sure you follow the rulebook like any parolee. That's right, I'm gonna be your worst fucking nightmare, sweetheart. Just sit in the chair and fill out the form," Ward said.

"Everything could be the same again. I got a kite the other day, sez my man Nesto, be coming home from soon."

"Another damn loser! He's nothing but a plantano. A loser like yourself," Ward said with disdain.

"We can set shit up again—"

"Yeah maybe. If I gave you chance. But I don't think I'm in a generous mood. You can't work for me. To tell the truth, Lil' Long, you're finished in this town. You're no longer useful to anybody. You pissed a lot of good people off when your stupid ass started killing for selfish reasons."

He brusquely ushered Lil' Long out the office.

"Hall, our man is on his way out," detective Kowalski said. His partner shifted his head from the coffee cup.

"Your man. If it was up to me, his ass would be in a pine box already."

"He still got some mileage left."

"Here we're trying to solve crime knowing he is a criminal. Man, I can't understand who is running this shit."

"Our job is to recruit him, sit back and wait. If you don't like it..."

"It's not a matter of if I like it. It's I don't understand the damn thing. This is not law and order."

"Hall, Hall, you sound like a pissed off rookie, who can't make a damn mook. Come on we're bigger than that. Just sitback and enjoy the movie. Hey, hey look at that cute Spanish number coming over there. Ah, that brings a smile to your face, huh?"

"That ain't enough ass for me. She sure got some nice lips," Hall said staring. "Maybe she could do some justice with them lips."

"You and me both brother," Kowalski whistled.

"Where's that lil' prick, dammit?"

"Taxi!"

"There he is. Our man has arrived..."

A gray sedan pulled to a stop in front of him. He hesitated then opened the car door and jumped in the back seat.

"Don't tell me you're nervous about this little trip." Hall greeted him.

"No I think he doesn't like our whip. Not your usual style, huh Michael?" Kowalski asked.

"Seat belts please. We are just in time, huh? Great and we know where you're going," Hall said.

"Wait up muthafuckas, all I was doing was trying to get a cab. This ain't no fucking cab—"

"You bet your bottom dollar, homey. We're giving your crippled ass a free ride home. Just sit back and enjoy. This one is on us," detective Kowalski said.

"So what da dealie, man? Why y'all rushing me for? Y'all arresting me or sump'n? If it ain't like that, y'all need to fall back! Just let me da fuck out, right now."

"I'm so sorry, it seems like our mannerisms does not seem to be getting the kind of reaction we thought we should get, Hall. Now let's try my plan. Plan B. Listen you fucking jerk, we're running this show. You are a nobody. And we're not gonna let you turn this into some sort of funky revenge for my dead brother's sequel. You're not gonna go around shooting anyone. You're not gonna rip the drug dealers off. No more extortion. Get my drift? And you're certainly, certainly not gonna take any more protection money from them. We will handle all that now. Our turf. Your job, I'll spell it out, is very important." Detective Kowalski barked at the passenger's fuming mug. Kowalski removed a cellular phone from his pocket and shoved it at the agitated passenger.

"What da..."

A fist to the backseat rider's mid-section ended his

protest. The blow left him coughing.

"Hey don't you fucking mess up the upholstery. We'll have you clean it with your tongue."

"Can't follow instructions," Kowalski said, looking at his fist.

The passenger turned to see the car pulled to a stop under an overpass. The door was flung open and the driver got out. His hand gripped his weapon. Then the detective was in his face shouting.

"Un-coach able, that's what's gonna be written on your tombstone," Hall said, peering down at the passenger wrenching in pain, then falling limp on the pavement. A boot made contact with his groin.

"What's it gonna be, my bitch or my nigga? Hold it a minute before you make your choice," Hall said, jumping between Kowalski and the passenger's hobbled body. "There is one more thing I want you to know before you make your choice. He'll do anything to kill you."

His grimace was met with another fist smashed into sore ribs. He sank to his knees on the asphalt. Detective Kowalski reared back to deliver a right cross. He saw it coming but could do nothing.

"Who did you think called the ambulance for you when you were shot?"

The question lingered for a beat.

"It was me," came the answer, accompanied by a blow to the side of Lil' Long's head. "Me, me you idiot. You owe me your life," the detective screamed.

"Hey easy, easy," Hall said as he grabbed Kowalski from

behind. "If you break his fucking jaw, he will not be able to talk. We want him to snitch, right?"

"Nah! You know what? Fuck this bastard. I don't need him to snitch for me. Let him fuck up your account, my man," Kowalski said holding the gun at his head.

"Aw c'mon who're you kidding? You've wanted... no you have desired him since day one. You saved his life. He owes you."

"Yeah, but not all fucked up like this, I mean..." Kowalski responded.

"Ya don't need good legs to be a damn snitch. All you need are headlights. He got them," Hall said, pointing at Lil' Long's eyes.

"Get comfy," Kowalski said. "We've got some demands, bitch."

He heard the release of zippers and saw Kowalski pulled his dick out trying to shove it in his mouth. Hall massaged his temple with the service Glock while taking pictures with a camera phone.

TWENTY-FIVE

Beaten down but defiant, Lil' Long dripping blood limped back to the building. It was dark, there were young kids hanging in the front of the building.

"Watch da fuck, where you running, shortie."

"You don't have to curse at me you know," he said helping Lil' Long to his feet. Lil' Long brushed himself off. The kid reached down and picked up the phone. He handed the phone to Lil' Long.

"My bad shortie. Keep the phone. It still got some minutes left on it. Go ahead you can call anywhere on it." Lil' Long limped away.

Lil' Long continued into the building. Blood from his ruptured sutures dripped on his uptown sneakers. Lil' Long reached his floor and entered his apartment. He rushed to the bathroom, found a towel. He used hot water to wet it then went into the bedroom. There, he fell on the bed writhing in pain, the hot towel draped around his wounds. Reaching for the telephone Lil' Long pressed speed dial #2 and put the phone call on speaker.

"What's popping, papi?"

"Tina, bust it. You need to get here right now. I'm twisted. These cops be... just come."

"Daddy, you don't want me to bring some arroz con pollo, the way you like it?"

"Nah, fuck da food. Bitch, you ain't on your way yet?"

The pain was so intense Lil' Long squirmed with each movement. He leaned over to the nightstand and pulled out a glass vial, emptied the contents into a pipe, then lit it. Lil' Long smoked the pipe until his eyelids were too heavy to keep open.

Tina used her keys to open the door. She walked to the bedroom where she found Lil' Long asleep but grunting and tossing as if in dream. She tried not to wake him. She searched his pockets and took him for a small amount of cash. Then she made herself comfortable and lit the pipe he once blazed. Once the effect was felt, she lay next to him and curled her body beside his. Remote in hand she switched the television on and channel surfed.

TWENTY-SIX

With the keys to his simple abode in his sweating hand, Rightchus hurried back to his apartment. He palmed a large piece of rock that he had scored and couldn't wait to light the stem. Rightchus had earned ends from snitching out Lil' Long and planned to soothe his mind. He pushed his key into the lock pushed on the door and it fell flat inside the apartment. Rightchus gasped and stared around, his eyes widened.

"Who da fuck?" He yelled and backed out the apartment. "If anybody's in there this is a warning, I got real big guns and I don't care who I kill..."

He waited, peeped inside, and then entered the apartment armed with a knife.

"What da fuck!"

Rightchus wore a perplexed stare and glanced at the set of keys in his hand. "Oh man, oh shit, those crazy Maruichis. Now the fucking landlord is gonna have ma muthafucking ass. No, he already has ma ass. He's gonna have my damn life."

He looked around shaking his head at his scattered wares. "I've got to get da fuck up out of here before that jerk, shit-head super finds me here."

Rightchus hustled about the place hastily retrieving the few belongings that mattered. Verbally checking each item.

"Now I gotta have my Beat Box with my demo tapes and the pictures of my seeds. Now, now where are those damn pictures of my precious children?" He examined them one by one while reflecting on the possibility of visiting his family. He quickly hit the block clutching his prize possessions and the scheme he hoped would put him back into the grace.

He would take the offer from the cops and at the same time keep Maruichi off his back. His steps quickened, then slowed as he neared the bus stop. He stood there and nodded at people he didn't know and watched them rush by.

TWENTY-SEVEN

Early in the morning, Lil' Long awoke, raised his head slightly and peered down below his waistline. There was no more bleeding. Gone were the pains. Lil' Long noticed Tina. He sighed as he watched his hardness disappear between the apple red lips of his shapely guest. Tina sucked and licked rigorously. Lil' Long groaned.

"Easy, Tina... Ahh... Oh yeah, take care, girl. Yeah, yeah," Lil' Long said.

His fingers were playing in Tina's bronzed streaked mane. She twitched her lips, moved her head around while her tongue stabbed at his scrotum. His love instrument was rock hard. Lil' Long could feel the inevitable explosion brewing on the horizon. Before the tidal rush exploded, the sexy Tina abruptly changed position.

She began rubbing her caramel color tits smoothly against his hardness. Using both hands, she then massaged her caramel breasts. Sensitive nipples hardened as her tongue snaked all over her juicy lips. She slid her tongue along Lil' Long's anxious throat. She worked deliberately and gently, moving away from the area of his crotch. Tina languidly licked every inch between. She teased the head continually, flicking her tongue back and forth. Each movement caused her tits to dance.

"Damn! That stiffy looks so good... So-o-o good," Tina whispered.

Her hot breath made Lil' Long quiver, suddenly she jumped on it. "Ahh yeah... hmm..." she wailed as she began to ride the muscular beast. Her breasts hopped up and down like a bunny rabbit.

"Ohh... Ahh oww. Nah you can't do it that hard bi-bi-bitch. That way gon' hurt 'em stitches. Turn around and do it the other way. Let me see that fat ass work."

Tina spun her body around, crouched until Lil' Long shuddered. His toes curled and then he screamed. Tina continued to hold on.

"Oh ah, oh oh-oh-oh. Ugh, yeah, yeah." Tina ground her pussy on the Lil' Long's huge dick. Tina arched her back and threw her head back bucking into climax. Lil' Long held onto the back of her mane. He could feel another explosion coming on.

Groping her own breast, she screamed, "Oh yesss... whew, papi. Ahh, papi."

"Yes bitch keep it moving, keep it moving. I'm about to... agh..."

"Oh yeah, baby. Ahh... that was a good one. Hmm... ha... ha... ha... ha..." Tina's voice trailed off to a soft chuckle.

She slowed her rocking to a steady grind and hissed.

She leaned forward playing with Lil' Long's feet and remained perched on top until he went limp.

"I need to get my hair done up, baby. Look what you did to it," she said rolling off and onto the floor.

"Ouch! Watch da fuck what you doing, bitch?"

"I'm sorry, boo. I mean I forgot you're still hurting," Tina kissed her hand, reached over and touched his groin area. "Your dick was like so rock inside me. Why, you weren't hurt-ing' then?" She reached over and kissed the area.

Lil' Long replaced the weapon under the pillow. Tina moved her ass around, tugged at the length of her hair and headed to the bathroom. Lil' Long remained motionless. His eyes were closed when the sound of toilet flushing ushered Tina back into the bedroom.

"Look at what you've done to my hair," she said in the best of her saddened tone. Lil' Long opened his eyes. He removed the money clip from the pocket of his jeans and stuffed a wad of bills at Tina's thonged ass. She counted the money with quickness.

"This is only a hundred a fifty," she declared.

"Yeah and? Go to the deli and get me some break-fast, girl."

"Where's the money?" Tina asked with her hand on her hip and palm out. Lil' Long eyeballed her. Tina was a sexy and exotic Latin girl. Her shapely figure made her hot.

"The money?" she prompted as Lil" Long continued to look. "You gotta pay for what you got and what you got is a high class ghetto bitch. I like expensive things. I don't come cheap. So if you're gonna be penny pinching then I just got to go get me another baller. A big baller. Feel me?" She was close up and in his face. Her hair touching his grill.

Lil' Long could smell the result of their sex. He reached up and parted her hair exposing her face. His finger played with her lips. Then he thrust his tongue in her mouth. She grunted and fell on top of him. Lil' Long rolled her over and eased his hardened member past thongs and into her fire.

"Ohh... Ohh... Ohh." She groaned.

"I want ham and cheese with fried eggs on a roll," whispered Lil' Long between strokes. "Holla if you hear me, girl."

"How do you want your eggs?" Tina asked. Her firm round derrière rising to meet his every stroke.

"Huh, uh... I want them hard," Lil' Long grunted and stroked to an orgasm. He rolled off.

"I've asked you before, where is the money? This here is to get my do did. So where is the money for your breakfast? Fork it over." Tina said as she dressed.

"Money," she said with her palms up.

"All right," Lil' Long said, reaching for additional bills. He peeled off a yard. "You straight now, bitch. You straight?"

"Why I got to be a bitch? Why can't a woman..." Tina saw Lil' Long reach under the pillow. Her mouth opened.

"I'm gone. I was just making a joke. I was gonna go. I was just playing. You know me, Lil' Long. It's whatever you want."

"Bring me some orange juice and a vanilla Dutch."

Tina took no chance. With the money for her hair secured in a Louis Vuitton Monogram handbag, Tina made the sign of the cross when she passed a church on her way to the bodega. Before she could give her order Tina spotted the detective car coming to a stop. On her way out she watched the officers get out of the car and head in the direction of the apartment building. She pressed her speed dial.

"Lil' Long you need to get the fuck up out of that crib already. Two DT's are on their way up." Tina hiked her tight skirt, waved her ass into the lucky cab and was gone.

TWENTY-EIGHT

"One free man walking!" a prison officer announced.

"Sign right here for your properties. You're a free man, son." The officer noted.

Ernesto De La Rosa heard the words and stepped proudly in his farewell march. He stopped, hugged a guard here, an inmate there. His Russian associate, Igor was happy to see him leave. He approached the nineteen-year-old with muscular arms outstretched. Their lengthy hug ended with Igor planting a kiss on both Ernesto's cheeks.

"From the bottom of my heart, Nesto want to thank you for all..." Igor waved his hand silencing Ernesto.

"You did this, you and only you. Don't waste your time in the streets with the girls. My sister will be expecting you," Igor smiled.

"We've got a great understanding of what you do, who you see, right? Don't try to fuck me. I still have a lot of eyes and ears out there for me. Do we understand each other

Ernesto?"

The three pats on the broad back of Igor served as confirmation.

"Nesto be good to the streets..."

"Be easy with the bitches..."

"Hope you learned your lessons and not be back up in this piece anytime soon..."

Ernesto De La Rosa stepped into freedom for the first time in three years with a chant.

"Nesto ain't never coming back, ya heard!"

TWENTY-NINE

"...And when you tell him be serious and don't let him out-talk you. Men love to try and do that shit," Josephine warned as Deedee made her way out the Range.

"Don't worry, I got this," Deedee yelled when she emerged decked-out in a simple, black dress. She walked determinedly into the building that housed her uncle's studio.

Eric Ascot was sitting at the controls and turned briefly. When he saw his niece, he quickly got up, greeted her with a kiss on the cheek, and led her to private lounge area.

"How's Josephine and..."

"She's fine but my question is why can't I hang out with Coco? I mean uncle you're treating her as if she's some kinda bad person..."

"Hon, listen we had this discussion before. Coco is not a bad person and I'm not trying to treat her that way, but whenever she comes around she brings trouble."

"That's not all together true uncle."

"Oh really..."

"I mean we've hung out and there was no trouble whatsoever."

"Yeah but if you weren't hanging tough with Coco and her crew we wouldn't..."

"Uncle E., what happened that night, I took responsibility for it. I did take the car without permission and..."

"Even so, it was due to them taking you about the place and then to some spot where only gangsters hang up in Harlem that caused all the problems..."

"I disagree, uncle. Coco is not a gangster. She's hard and she's from the hood but she's no gangster."

"I see her showing colors all the time. She's got her red bandana. That's why I'll probably let her work with Show Biz. He'll probably do a better job, make a better record..."

"Wow, just like that uh Uncle. Uncle did you know she was arrested, the detectives have hounded her and not once has she changed her story. She's played along, kept her mouth shut and for that she gets dumped." Deedee stared at her uncle in search of a reaction.

"She also wears blue bandanas, green and yellow, usually they match her sneaks."

"She's been harassed by the police and never changed the story, huh? You know what, take Big Jake and Mack along with you. And don't be hanging up in Harlem all night long," Eric said, then hugged and kissed his niece.

"Thanks uncle E.," Deedee said.

They walked out of the private lounge area and went on the elevator. Eric rode with his niece and walked her to the waiting Range.

"Hi Mr. Ascot," Josephine greeted them when they reached the vehicle.

"C'mon Josephine, how many times must I say this, its Eric. Later for all the formalities. How long have you been living with us... huh?"

"My bad. I know since I've been here I've only seen you like twice or maybe three times. I haven't seen you enough to determine how I'm gonna call you."

They continued walking to where two beefy men stood next to a Range Rover and a Mercedes. As they approached, Eric addressed the men.

"Mack you and Big Jake go with the girls." Eric said.

He hugged and kissed the girls. Deedee led the way into the luxury SUV.

"I'll get Sam to come around if I need him. Be cool, I'll see y'all later," Eric waved as the Range rolled out.

When they arrived uptown, the girls stood outside the legendary Apollo Theater enjoying a busy sidewalk scene. Coco, decked in Baby Phat blue jeans and red T-shirt, and white Nike Air Force Ones with red and blue laces, walked up on them.

"You did say three? Am I late or sump'n yo?" Coco asked checking her two-way pager. They stopped on the busy sidewalk and quickly became the center of attraction. "So what's popping girl?" Coco screamed and hugged Josephine, then she air-kissed Deedee.

"Stop playing, Dee. Is that the whip, yo? Your uncle let you...?" Coco asked as she pointed to the vehicle.

"Yep, it's my uncle's idea..." Deedee started but Coco interrupted.

"It's even more tricked out way pass the nines, yo."

"Coco lemme tell you, girl," Josephine added. "It's got chromed shoes, wheels spinning even when it's not moving.

"Oh lemme find out, y'all pimpin', yo," Coco yelled.

"What you can hear the Bose theater system thumping in thurr?" Josephine said.

"My uncle just added a few more things to it..."

"Oh it be some good shit right thurr, girlfriend," Josephine said.

A grin slowly overpowered the tension on Coco's grill. She instinctively reached for the door handle. As soon as she did, the door was released opened. Coco with a smile of surprise gave Deedee a high-five.

"Oww! This my kinda whip, yo."

They entered through the backdoor when the steps emerged, automatically. Coco felt the speakers vibrate the interior of the luxury SUV.

> *Damn why they wanna stick me for my papers?*
>
> *Damn why they wanna stick me for my papers?*

The Notorious B.I.G. pondered through the lyrics of his song. Deedee and Coco wedged themselves into the comfort of plush leather seats. Two round-bald heads occupying the front seats, nodded in sync to the heavy bass-line of a Hip Hop classic. Suddenly one of the baldheads turned to the other and said:

"Best rapper to ever did bless us." Their noggins moving in sync, provided the necessary affirmation.

"This Mack and you remember Big Jake, they're my bodyguards," Deedee said to Coco.

"Your bodyguards, they're feeling Biggie, yo," Coco said, starting to sing along.

"Just listening to you rapping along with B.I.G., wow Coco... it just shows your talent, girl. You know what?"

"No, what yo?" Coco asked, eyeing the screens on the back of the headrest.

"If you two could've ever done something together," Deedee said. She paused in deep thought then recovered in time to add. "Whoa Coco, that would've been platinum, for real. Shoot, double platinum, at least."

"If you think so, that's peacel ain't stressin'. I can't wait to take my shot," Coco said.

"Are you doing any live shows?" Josephine asked.

Coco thought for a minute then answered.

"I don't know if you're down but I might do a show next week with Geo and..."

"Which Geo? You mean Spanish Geo?" Josephine asked.

"You know the one. I want you to perform too Jo, but don't be messing with any of them men, they all got girls, yo."

"And them bitches love to fight..." Deedee said.

"I don't care. I'll go and perform. But I can't help it if

their mens and them be feelin' me." Josephine smiled.

The Range rolled amidst heavy traffic. The girls made their way to the Jamaican Hot Pot. Traffic slowed when they turned on Seventh Ave. Further down they came to a dead stop. Deedee peered out from her dark glasses. She watched a small group of curious onlookers as they milled in a casual manner. Her French manicured tips touched the control and released the window next to her.

"Rightchus doing his thing again," Coco said.

"Let's walk down the block the restaurant is only couple blocks away." Josephine suggested. "It's such a nice day..."

THIRTY

The girls sat in the restaurant enjoying the culinary specialties from the island. The soft, jazzy licks from a piano accompanied by lively steel-drums, floated through the air.

"This place is tiny but really nice and cozy. They should think of expanding," Deedee said glancing around the eatery.

"Anyway, so your furniture arrived, huh..."

"Oh yeah. I was surprised, the delivery people set up all the stuff," Coco said.

"How does it look?" Deedee asked.

"It's good. I like it, yo."

"Did your mom liked it too, Coco?" Josephine asked.

"You know madukes," Coco deadpanned.

"I know what you mean, girl. I'm divorcing mine on account of how she harassed the stockings off me on the plane ride going back to Charleston."

ANTHONY WHYTE

"You and your mother just need to be away from each other right now," Deedee said.

"Parents be trippin'. They don't be thinking or even looking out for they kids, they all about themselves..."

"Yeah I hear you, I hear you. Like I wanna spank madukes. It's like I have to make decisions for her."

"It's like you have got to have back-up parents. I'm glad my uncle was there and..."

"Word-up, give thanks and praises..."

"Why you getting all religious and shit, yo?"

They high-fived and laughed as the distinct aroma of spicy Curry Goat and Oxtail floated from the kitchen to the girls' table. The waiter placed the orders in the respective positions with peas and rice, along with fried plantains on the side. The girls held hands and Josephine gave thanks.

"The last time Uncle E., brought me here, I'm telling you, I drank like a gallon of water with the spicy meal. It's good," Deedee said. "You better get a soda or..."

"Nah, I know what to get. Let's order the island punch, yo."

"Island punch? Is that like ah... the Rum Punch? Uncle E. had that the last time. He made faces like it was bitter. Island Punch, Coco? What's that?" Deedee asked.

"That's that stuff to knock you out, yo."

"I'll try it. Shoot, I'm not driving tonight," Deedee said and raised her hand to get the waiter's attention. "I'll order..."

"So what's new? Have y'all decided on any colleges?" Coco asked.

"I've narrowed it down to about six. No four," Deedee said.

"I don't know. I don't know if I really wanna go to college right away. I really don't know," Josephine said.

When the girls left the restaurant they saw the bodyguard in the Range Rover nodding to the music, thumping block party style. They got in the SUV. Josephine pulled out a small jar with green weed. She peeled the cigar, replaced the content with weed from the jar and rolled the tobacco leaf into a neat blunt. She smoothed then sparked it. Puffed twice and passed it. Coco took the blunt and caught herself before taking a toke. She passed it on.

"Yo, y'all smoke, I'd love to, but I can't. I gotta have clean specimen, yo."

"C'mon Coco, they ain't gonna know. Just this one time," Josephine pleaded but Coco lit a cigarette instead.

"Them oye on the block be selling that in a jar. That shit is potent, got all the heads hooked, yo."

"You know everything about the street, don't you? Is that is where all your inspiration comes from?" Deedee asked.

"Inspiration? In terms of what?" Coco asked and passed up the drag when the blunt came back to her.

"For your rhymes and..."

"Some, but I deal with my problems. Like madukes and her drug shit, ya know?"

"And she does have the drug shit down," Josephine said.

"Don't be talking shit about madukes. What about your parents, yo? You said your dad's a base head too."

"I want my boobs to be bigger," Josephine said changing the subject.

"It's my right to have a breast enlargement if I want."

"But why ah..." Deedee started staring at her incredulously.

"This bitch is fuckin Looney toon. Why are you even gonna be bothered with that bullshit. You know you gotta go and get an examination and..."

"I already had all the preliminaries done. I want this," Josephine confessed.

"But why I still don't get it. Some guy told you," Deedee started but Josephine cut her off.

"This has nothing to do with guys, this is for me. I wanna look real sexy. C'mon girls, you're either with or not. I've just been thinking about it that's all. Y'all ain't gotta lose yourself over it."

They laughed benefiting from the inebriating effect of their high. Their bodies swayed from the aftermath of the alcohol.

"Were you ever like not proud of your mother? I mean..." Deedee began. She watched Coco light a cigarette and saw smoke rushing from Coco's lips.

"There were times when I've had to completely flip on Madukes, yo," Coco responded.

"Flipped on her like how, Coco?" Josephine asked.

"I mean there are times when she ain't acting right, you know? Madukes is Madukes. She has her rights. But times when she be straight messing up, yo. I got to step to her like, 'look ma, that shit ain't tight. You know?' She be frontn' like Scooby Doo."

"Yeah, that's the reason I'm trying so desperately to find my mother," Deedee said. "I was ashamed of my mother. No, make that *very* ashamed of her. She was a crack-head. Damn, how low can you go? I wanna find my mother soon. Maybe she could see me, *her daughter* walking across the stage with my high school diploma."

"Yo, graduation is six weeks away. What if you don't find her? You still got to go forward with your life," Coco said.

"I guess..."

"It's cool, yo. Don't sweat it." Coco said listening to the soulful dirge of Lauren Hill's *Ooh la-la*. The lament of Fugee's La expanded cloudlessly through the speakers.

THIRTY-ONE

It was seven in the evening. The girls heard ranting from behind them. They turned and saw Rightchus approaching the door of the parked Range. The bodyguards stepped to the front. Rightchus pulled out a long knife.

"Coco, Deedee. My, my what are you two beautiful beings doing here? Who's that? Don't tell me, Josephine, what's goin' on y'all? I ain't seen you in a minute."

"Hi," Josephine said.

"Sorry to burst your bubble but we gotta go, Mr. Rightchus," Deedee said.

"I gotta get da fuck up, yo?" Coco exclaimed.

"Everyone is in a hurry. I'm in a hurry too if I didn't have them Maruichi boys after my ass, I'd be cool. I didn't know the shit wasn't real. It ain't my damn fault. It's them cheap ass drug dealers dancing up an' down on da product."

"Yo, what da fuck you yapping' bout nigga? We ain't got

time to yap about no coke, Wop. I gotta be gone like yesterday."

"Yeah, I feel you," Rightchus said putting away the chop-
per. "I mean, shoot, we need to conversate on lots of subjects.
I'm a person with all kinds of knowledge. Great minds think
alike feel me, Coco? But I'm saying, what is da real science,
girl?"

"Rightchus don't start with that bullshit..."

"Ahight, ahight, I hear you, I hear you girl. Well, in ref-
erence to that, I wanna say, I don't wanna start fucking with
y'all young girls anyways, cuz I always gets fucked around,
see? I'm not having my shit screwed up on y'alls' account.
Every time I get around y'all young chickens, shit happens.
Bullets start flying, people dropping. I don't get down like that.
Speaking of dropping, I've seen the walking dead..."

"You and everybody else living in these parts, yo," Coco
said, interrupting Rightchus.

"Then you know what I'm dealing with, Coco?"

"'The Walking Dead' isn't that a scary movie?" Deedee
asked, cutting off Rightchus's explanation.

"I could tell y'all ain't serious. Peeps all the time wanna
run up on a nigga, ya kno, reason why I'm here is cuz me an
some fuckin' peeps at war ya kno. Can't go home an' all. But
I'm build me a MTV crib with bullet proof everything, all in
time, still..." Rightchus said.

"All right Mr. Rightchus we gotta be moving on..." The
bodyguard pushed Rightchus as he spoke.

"Nah, don't do that. A muthafucka can't be takin' aim
over here. I can see y'all just right. What y'all should be more

interested in is the muthafucka I be seein'. Saw him. Yesterday... last night. Hmm twenty-four hours later, things tend to get fuzzy. Old age."

"Negative. Too much drugs. Your brains fried. Gone out to lunch, yo."

"Coco, you can keep spitting all that b.s. But I'm telling you girl, you need to put me down. Me da Shawty Wop, cuz I've seen him. I've seen da nigga," Rightchus said.

"Seen who, yo?" Coco asked. She threw her hands in the air, perplexed.

"I've seen him," repeated Rightchus. He took a couple steps back and noticed the security team moving in front of the girls.

Coco and Deedee stood close to the security team, Josephine stood next to the Range. Rightchus was in his flow. "I'm saying, I've seen him, I've seen dude..."

"Who is this fool talking 'bout, yo?"

"Lil' Long, that's who."

Silence like an eagle, descended swallowing the atmosphere and leaving each girl with cold feet. There was a power to ruthlessness on the street. It was visible when the mention of a name conjured fear. The girls slowly acknowledged Rightchus's urgency. The mention of his name was a reminder of a brutal period in the girls' experiences. He had preyed on many victims and was responsible for the deaths of Coco's friends. He and his friend, Vulcha had savagely raped and assaulted Deedee.

"I thought he was dead. Wasn't he killed in the shootout at Deedee's uncle? I was there. And he was spitting up lead and all that, yo,"

"Yeah, I know, I know. I thought he was dead," Deedee said.

"Yeah, you and everybody else, right? But un'nerstan', I'm sayin' I seen da nigga. He doubled up like he got a hunch-back or sump'n. I'm sayin' I seen him, I seen da muthafucka. You kno'? He be wearing dark shades covering his eyes, limpin'. I'm tellin' da truth. Coco, he knows, he knows. He limped away and broke out as soon as I was getting ready to step to him. Feel me? I'm Rightchus Allah. I'm da mu'fuckin' Shawty Whopper. And y'all know that whopping ain't even easy. Peeps be acting cheesy, and all. But you know what?"

"What?" Coco and Deedee asked simultaneously.

"When I hit you, I hit you with da raw truths. No lies or tales follow my word, cuz my word is bond."

"Rightchus, Rightchus, listen we're not sweating Lil' Long. We gotta be out, so hear me out. If Lil' Long wanna jump, he'll catch the worst beat-down of his life. And it's for ignorant people like him that we've got bodyguards. Know what I mean, yo?" Coco said.

"Matter o' fact, word on da streets is that his man Nesto is cominng from up-north soon. And Coco; they got tight when they were locked up together. Let me get down with y'all. I'll supervise them big boys for you. I'll keep it on the down low. Them dumb bodyguards; ain't got a thing on da Shawty Wop. I'll wop a mu'fucka so fast, his family be hurting," Rightchus said as he shuffled his feet, shadow boxing.

"Rightchus, please stop. Just stop it alright. Chill before something really does go down, yo," Coco said.

"Please, before you hurt yourself," Deedee added.

A gunshot sounded somewhere close. Rightchus took off down the street.

"We're all good? What happened to Shawty?" One of the bodyguards asked.

"Man, I don't know, yo. Homey said he had beef with Maruichi peoples. I don't know, yo."

"Who were those guys?" Deedee asked.

"Should we check if he is dead or what?" Josephine asked.

"Nope, I think we should bounce, yo. No use getting involved with this nigga, he might be hot. Fuck around and get shot," Coco said then she turned at the bodyguards. "Y'all could check if y'all want. But I'm out, yo." The bodyguards hesitated for a second.

"Don't make sense sticking your nose in other people's business." One of the bodyguards said as he put his gun away.

"Everybody in the set's good. Then we fittin' to go," the other said. They peeled out.

"You know my uncle said every time I'm around you, bullets start flying. I had to argue with him and that's why he sent the bodyguards."

"Look, it will be all right, you can drop me at the cab stand or sump'n. Don't bug on Rightchus's account. It was his ass they were busting at," Coco said.

THIRTY-TWO

Deedee and Josephine walked into the apartment. They were still woozy from the alcohol and weed. Both wandered into the kitchen and sat down. They were drinking juice and watching television.

"It was cool to hang out with Coco. There's always so much drama," Josephine said.

"All that drinking zapped my energy. I gotta go find my bed. My head is spinning. I feel soo sleepy," Deedee yawned.

"Yeah me too, I'm right behind you," Josephine said going into the bathroom. "This is such a huge place I still can't remember where stuff is."

Later, Josephine sat down at the kitchen table and dialed her cell phone. "Daddy this is your daughter, Jo. When you have a chance, please call me back, thank you." As soon as she had put the phone away, Eric Ascot walked in.

"Hey Mr., I mean Eric. How're you?"

"Hey Josephine I'm fine. You didn't hang out with Dee?"

"Yep we did, but Coco has a curfew and she had to be home early so we..."

"Oh Dee, she's here?"

"Yeah, I think she's asleep."

Ascot was already upstairs checking for Deedee. He walked back downstairs and went to the refrigerator, got a beer and popped it open. Earlier he had paid his tribute to Maruichi while having a few drinks with him. Now he just wanted to kick back and fall asleep. Josephine was feeling loquacious.

"Josephine you've got a nice body. If I were you, I would-n't worry too much about making any changes just yet. Maybe after you've had a couple children or so. Maybe then," Eric said and opened another beer.

"Eric, my tits are soo small and they come with these big chunky nipples. My nipples are as big as the rest of my breast. It's soo embarrassing. That's the reason I never played sports. I like buying beach outfits but I've got to buy an extra small top. I wish I had some of the fat from my ass up here." Josephine said rubbing her rump and then her breast. She fondled them over clothes.

Eric stared at her in disbelief. She started to unbutton her top.

"See I don't even have to wear a bra. Do you like 'em, Eric?" She asked sadly revealing her breasts. Eric's jaw fell open and his lips became moistened from salivating. He was about to retreat but Josephine didn't give him a chance. She walked over closer to him.

"Take a better look. See how big my nipples are, Eric?"

"Ah Josephine..." His breath became shallow. He

choked on the beer and then the bottle almost fell. Eric struggled with his feelings. Eric felt his hands go clammy. He glanced away and nervously sipped the brew.

"See, you don't like them either. You don't even wanna look at them. They are ugly aren't they too?"

"Nah, that's not it. I..."

"What is it?" Josephine asked. "Do you wanna see the rest of my body? You wanna compare, Eric?"

Josephine began to disrobe. Shocked, Eric watched as the affable teen with a voluptuous body blithely undressed.

"Jo, ah, Josephine you've got to get yourself together, here. Get your clothes back on," Eric said. All the liquor he had drank was making him confused.

"Nobody wants me and I think it's all because of my tits. See the rest of my body, what do *you* think?" Josephine said in her most pitiful tone.

"I think you should put your clothes back on, Josephine. Beauty is from within and no one can take that away," Eric protested as Josephine came so close he could reach out and touch her. Eric examined her body with his eyes.

"How's the rest of me compared to my breasts?"

Eric knew things were getting out of control when his breathing went shallow and he had problems swallowing. He watched her hands roaming aimlessly over her body.

"You're very easy, much easy on anyone's eyes, kid," he said smiling uneasily.

"Kid? Is that's what you think because I don't have big boobs right," she asked dejectedly.

"No, no, no way that's not what I meant..." Eric had moved closer to reassure Josephine.

"I could see that you were disgusted," she said.

"Nah, nah, Josephine. Don't take it like that," he said touching and feeling her warm skin against his hand. Her body trembled.

"What I meant was that you're beautiful," Eric smiled nervously.

Josephine took his hand from her face and placed it on her shoulder. The next second, Eric's face was burrowed between her breasts sucking and fingering.

"We shouldn't, ah... we..."

"Oh but don't stop, please don't stop Eric..." Josephine hummed pleasurably. Her body shuddered all over from the teasing of his tongue and his groping hands. She unbuttoned his shirt. His mouth opened to speak and she muffled him with a kiss. Josephine sucked his lower lip into her mouth while they made out. She squirmed and tugged at his zip. Seconds later, he sat wearing only boxers on a chair.

Josephine used her tongue to spar with his as she pinched his nipples hard. Then she got down on her knees and let the tip of her tongue slid up and down Eric's thickened shaft. His body was tingling from her wet lips brushing against the length of his dick. She caressed his package and kneaded it until his incredible erection pointed to the ceiling. She rubbed the tip against her soft moistened, hot, love-box, squatting easily, she slid up and down his shaft. He set her desire on fire when he licked her areola in a circular motion.

Josephine moaned and moved her ass around. She

moved faster and faster. Then she was biting his shoulders to keep from screaming.

"Ooh, agh, yeah oh yes. Give it to me give it all to me. I can feel it in my belly oh yes!" Josephine exclaimed sucking hard on his neck and moving faster.

Eric eased her back on the top of the table and Josephine raised her legs high. Her whole body quaked when he licked her toes as his stroke reached deep inside her. Spread eagle on the kitchen table, Josephine was filled with delight. Eric pounded her inside and she raised her ass to greet his every thrust. His hips moved faster and faster.

"Ugh ah, yes oh I'm coming!"

"Yes Eric that feels so good come for me baby!"

He busted deep inside her, his body jerked from the ejaculation.

"Ahh..." Josephine sighed. "That was soo good. Let's do it again."

"Yeah, I don't think so. We'll wake Dee, for sure," Eric said.

"I'll be quiet." Josephine promised. She kissed Eric again.

"Let's take it upstairs," he said with a smile.

"Okay, okay it's your call, Eric." Josephine said. Quietly they made their way up the short flight of stairs and into Eric's bedroom.

THIRTY-THREE

Monday morning came too quickly for Coco. She slammed the door and raced down the stairs to the street. Recklessly, she dashed across the street to the bus stop just in time to be the last one on the bus. After hanging with her girls this weekend, she was determined not to let anyone hold her back from getting her education. Coco stayed attentive throughout class time. Lunchtime didn't come quickly enough. Coco wandered through the hall and heard the familiar yakking of Josephine.

"Oh you just gonna walk past us like that, huh girlfriend. What we ain't good enough for you?"

"You know I don't even know why they let your Ghetto ass up in here," Coco said with a laugh. They walked out the building. Deedee slipped her shades on before speaking.

"I was thinking this morning about Rightchus and what he said about you know who..."

"I keep telling you don't let that shit bother you. I mean

no doubt you gonna be careful, but I think when it's your time to go, there's nothing that can be done..."

"On the real though, yo, we can't let bullshit like what Rightchus dealing with throw us off our tracks. I mean I know I've gotta graduate, cuz that's what we're all here for. So I'm saying from Rightchus to Lil' Long to po-po, ain't no one stopping Coco from reaching her goals."

"Here, here, that's a good rhyme right thurr. I love the way you say it right thurr..."

"You know what Coco, you're absolutely right and I don't think I should let these things get in my way, but you know by now, I'm a worry wart."

"I kind a agree," Josephine rejoined.

"Beg to second that," Coco added.

"Well whatever. I have to worry some about this Lil' Long character, I really don't want him to start any war with any of us."

"I hear you, Dee," Josephine said. "You're preaching that good gospel. Why that nigga want y'all so bad?"

"From the time Danielle was killed, he's been after us," Coco said.

"What he thinks y'all killed his man Vulcha?"

"It's not even that. That nigga thinks we set him up and tried to kill him. We should've really murdered his ass, yo," Coco said.

"After what he did to Dee, both him and his man should be killed," Josephine opined.

"I'm telling you though if that nigga thinks he could just

be around and we should be hiding, well I won't."

"We should just find his ass right, and... no we should dress up and play him take him to the mo and cut his dick off and watch him bleed to death..."

"See I told you, you're insane in the brain, bitch."

"I ain't playin'. What he gon do without his dick, huh?" Josephine asked. "He'd be like: Yo ma, I really want to fuck you but I got no dick..."

"Stop laughing Dee, you're encouraging this crazy-ass bitch, here."

"So Coco you could ride with us later, alright. You're gonna visit Miss Katie after school, right?" Deedee asked.

"You know I am. As long as she's in there I'm visiting. But my mother..."

"We'll take her too dammit. There's strength in numbers," Josephine said.

THIRTY-FOUR

Lil' Long dialed from the pay phone. There was a pause then a rustled voice was heard on the other end.

"Ward here," the voice said.

"Hello, what's good PO?" Lil' Long said. A crooked, sardonic grin spreading on his face.

"Your crippled ass better have a good reason for calling me. What do you want? Make it quick. I have no time for losers."

"I got sump'n you'll be interested in good buddy. Sump'n really big. Really, really big," Lil' Long sounded like he couldn't contain himself.

"I don't have time for all this clowning. You're wasting taxpayers' money by being on the phone. Come down to the office."

"Nah, don't trust 'em cops. Them muthafuckas rough me up so much; I'm still aching from the last time. I ain't fuckin' 'roun' there no mo'."

"Then what're you gonna do?"

"Meet me somewhere. I'll show and prove what I'm dealing wid. I promise, my man."

"I don't have time for your fun and games, chump."

"This ain't bout no fun and games, my man. You either want this info or you don't. There's a lot a shit ready to jump off. You want inside action or you want to read it in the newspapers?"

"This better be worth me getting out of my office."

"It will be worth it. It's something really big. Really, really big. It involves these Russians and these Spanish niggas and all that ya heard me. I'm telling you're gonna make a name for yourself off this one. This gon make you famous, you'll be the chief or sump'n. Ahight partner, this gon be some bulletproof type partnership from now on. Just show a nigga some love when you reach the top, alright man?"

"Alright, alright, get off the phone. I'll meet you at three pm over by the basketball courts."

"One-forty-seventh and Seventh? Thursday okay? You got it, ahight."

Lil' Long hung up the line and a smile enveloped his mug. He hobbled over to the bed in Tina's apartment and switched the television on. Lil' Long rubbed his fingers along the muzzle of his guns. He checked the magazines in both the Desert Eagles, filled. Lil' Long cocked the Desert Eagles and licked his lips to prevent over salivating. He grinned and replaced them.

THIRTY-FIVE

Monday evening after school, Coco along with Deedee and Josephine chatted while they rode to the hospital.

"I got to come along with you to visit Miss Katie," Deedee said.

"Oh you should as soon as she gets out of the coma I'll..."

"If she's still in a coma that's not good," Josephine said.

"What you think it won't change, huh?"

"I'm just saying the longer you stay in a coma is the less chance...?"

"Nah, don't even sweat it like that, Miss Katie, she's fighter. She ain't gonna give up. I mean she'll be all right, ahight yo?"

"You actually talk with her, Coco?" Josephine asked.

"The nurse thinks it's a good idea. So I just be kickin' it with her like she can hear me."

"Like what topics you be kickin' with her?"

"Please, any and everything. If you run into my mother out here, please don't mention Rightchus or Lil' Long. I mean she'll freak if she know anything like that. And don't talk any..."

"...Boys, hanging out or clubs. Talk about school, what college you're going to attend..."

"Oh you're trying to say you heard it all before, yo?"

"Don't worry girlfriend I won't mention anything. I got your back," Deedee said jokingly.

"See, you're joking around but that's for real, yo. My mother will flip if you start talking 'bout boys and stuff like that. What, it's got to be about edumication and all that, yo."

"I guess she feels that's the best way to keep your focus, right Coco?" Josephine asked jokingly.

"I'm focused bitch. Yo, madukes she was always about things like, 'friends ain't gonna last but a good education will.' She's always pushing complete high school and go to college."

"She should be satisfied I mean you're gonna graduate. She'll be there to see you," Josephine said.

"Yeah, but madukes will always see me as her little daughter. And after what went down with my arrest and all, I suppose she is trying to show that she cares about me. Plus, like now, she's around me on the day to day. Oh, that makes her even more curious, if that's possible."

"How long do y'all visit Miss Katie for?" Deedee asked.

"I don't know, maybe an hour or less, for the past three weeks."

The Range Rover sped to a stop in front of the hospital. Coco waved and walked to the entrance of the hospital.

THIRTY-SIX

Coco met her mother inside the hospital like she had been doing for the past three weeks. Her mother appeared happy and Coco hoped to hear good news of Miss Katie.

"Ma, you look like you heard sump'n good. What's...?"

"Oh Coco I'm so proud of you," Mrs. Harvey gushed.

"You are at the top of your class. You are the number one in all the scores and grades. Coco I dunno what to say..."

Coco reached over and hugged her mother. In each other's embrace, they walked silently to the elevator. Mrs. Harvey was beaming when she walked into Miss Katie's room.

"Oh Miss Katie," Rachel began to speak enthusiastically. "Coco did a great thing. She has the highest average in the school and she has turned in all her papers. She could be vale-dictorian. Oh Miss Katie if only you could see the letter from the school, you would be smiling and saying..."

"Lemme see the letter," Coco said interrupting her

mother.

"I'm really, really proud of you Coco. They thought that you weren't gonna make it and you just showed them non-believing asses up. I love that and I love the fact that you is my flesh and blood," Mrs. Harvey said.

Coco stared in guarded surprise at her mother's glowing face.

They heard a sound that surprised them both. It was a clearing of a raspy throat. Wide eyed with surprise Coco and her mother glanced at each other for a moment. Disbelief, then joy overcame them.

"Miss Katie!" They both shouted at the same time.

"Miss Katie, oh God bless you so," Rachel Harvey said through her tears. Miss Katie signaled for a glass of water. Coco quickly grabbed the cup next to her bed. Miss Katie drank. Her face made a smile and Coco moved closer.

"Oh Miss Katie..." Coco's emotions overcame her. She held Miss Katie's hand and her tears came.

"Coco don't cry girl. We all gotta go sometime," Miss Katie said in a faint voice. Her lips were parched and Coco smoothed them with Vaseline. She then gave her more water to drink.

"Shouldn't we get the nurse?"

"Doctors and nurses what they know anyways? Only God have the answers," Miss Katie proclaimed.

"Miss Katie, you heard us?"

"I know your mother was in a good mood..."

"Oh Miss Katie, I've been coming here all the time waiting for this and here..." Coco stopped speaking when Miss Katie started coughing. "Maybe we should call the nurse or a doctor. I think we should Miss Katie," Coco said anxiously.

"Now you know everything in the medical book is wrong with me. I've been up before this. This morning was the first time... briefly... ah.. ahem..." Miss Katie's voice trailed off.

"Miss Katie I'm gonna get a doctor or a nurse," Mrs. Harvey said and quickly left the room.

"Your mommy still crazy," Miss Katie said showing her teeth when her eyes reopened. "Coco you're gonna be a star, child. But you've got to respect elders. Read the Bible, embrace humility. Put God before you, Coco whatever you don't see God will. I want you to be strong for you and your mother. I know you'll be, but I feel I should tell you anyway." Miss Katie said. She held a slight smile on her face. Miss Katie's voice went silent and she closed her eyes.

"Miss Katie, Miss Katie..." Coco cried.

Miss Katie's eyes slowly opened. She took a breath and the pumps on the respiratory machine moved up and down.

"Is it supposed to be doing that?"

"It does what it feels like. Your mother should have pressed on the knob right here. The nurses would be here already."

"They're coming, they're coming Miss Katie, I can hear footsteps."

"Oh don't worry 'bout that. Coco you've gotta be the strength. Your work is not yet done, hon. You're gonna be a great person. Thank God I got to know you, Coco." Miss Katie's voice trailed off again. She closed her eyes as the nurse and Mrs. Harvey walked into the room.

Coco stared in disbelief as the nurse checked Miss Katie. The nurse eventually asked the visitors to wait outside in the hallway. Two doctors rushed past Coco and scurried inside the room. She knew it was bad when they later walked out of the room shaking their heads.

"Are you next of kin?" One of the doctors asked and the other walked away. "I'm afraid... there was nothing else we could've done... Katie Patterson ah... died a few minutes ago."

"Noooo!" Coco screamed her knees buckling. She wept with extraordinary violence, keening and howling. Her mother tried to steady her.

"This will calm her down," the nurse promised giving Coco a cup of water.

When she got home, Coco sat in the kitchen with her headphones on staring into space. She was numb to calls and text messages.

THIRTY-SEVEN

The next morning, Coco tarried at home, not wanting to go to school. Her mother tried to get her out of bed twice but both times Coco just pulled the covers further over her head and buried herself deeper seeking comfort in her dreams.

"Coco you've gotta go to school. Wake up, girl. You know Miss Katie wouldn't want you laying up in no bed just..." Mrs. Harvey begged. "Doggone you Coco. You've got to go to school now, girl c'mon get up."

Slowly, Coco dragged herself into the bathroom.

"See ya later, mom." Coco yelled and was out the door.

She managed to catch the bus. Coco knew she was moving but her mind was in a fog. She spent the morning session at school in a shell, functioning on autopilot. Josephine caught up to her smoking a cigarette at lunch.

"What's good Coco? You look like it's the day after..." Josephine said covering her mouth with her hands.

"I'll be ahight, yo. Just give me a few minutes," Coco requested. Josephine knew something was seriously wrong. She had never caught Coco crying before.

"Oh my God, I'm so sorry. Soo sorry oh..." Josephine's voice was shaky. She reached out and embraced Coco. They hugged and sobbed together.

"She was like a mother to me... Jo, she was fam," Coco whispered.

"I know y'alls relationship was real and tight, Coco. God bless her soul."

Lil' Long watched their movements from the back of a cab. He wanted to make an attempt at the girls but changed his mind when he saw the gray sedan parked across the street from the school. The occupants were also observing the girls.

THIRTY-EIGHT

Igor had arranged for Ernesto to meet his sister Karin Von Wink upon his release. She was married and ran a modeling agency. Igor assured Ernesto that she would provide him with a legal job. The image of being around models motivated Ernesto to get out of bed. He was ready to take the first step. The deal would be complete when Igor contacted him.

The train arrived at the midtown station. Ernesto alighted to the New York bustle of spring sidewalk madness, vendors and pedestrians competing for space. Ernesto headed to the Von Wink Agency, glancing into storefronts and at ladies strolling by.

A thin pale-skinned girl handed him a cold glass of water. "You can have sparkling water if you like. Karin is expecting you, go right in." She directed him straight ahead. Ernesto accepted the water and felt the stare on his ass. He knocked on the door.

"Come on in," an inviting voice called from the other side of the door. Ernesto walked into the office. There were several poster size pictures of gorgeous models decorating the wall but none was as striking as the red-haired woman sitting behind the glass-covered desk.

"Strip," she ordered.

Ernesto cocked his head to the side.

"Mr. De La Rosa are you going to stand there and play bashful, or are you going to comply," Karin queried in an all about business tone.

"No, no. I'm not here to be a model. I'm here to get a job, you know?"

"Ernesto, you're making this complicated. You get out of your clothes here and now. It could be worth making anywhere from ten thousand to the sky's the limit as a fashion model. We've got a show every week. Sometimes overseas. I don't know what my brother told you, but this is a modeling agency. We market pretty faces and nice bodies. The two doesn't always come in the same package. We've got to see the goods. It makes business sense."

"All right," Ernesto said, getting out of his jeans and T-shirt. He kicked off his boots. And stood in only his boxers.

"Everything off. Everything," Karin said.

Ernesto complied.

"Very nice," Karin said.

"You're clean," Karin said as she rubbed Ernesto's six-pack. "Any diseases or infections?"

"No."

"Very well. For insurance purposes I'll have my assistant schedule an appointment for a full medical examination."

"Mr. De La Rosa, you may get dressed."

Ernesto almost toppled to the floor while rushing to get back in his clothes.

"Have a seat, Mr. De La Rosa. Have you ever done any type of modeling? Been involved in any porn movies or any such thing?"

At the end of the interview, Karin rose.

"Mr. De La Rosa, it has been nice to meet you." Karin handed him some papers. "Take these forms with you and fill them out. Bring them on Saturday afternoon. There is a show and I want you to be seen. Any questions?"

Ernesto wore a smile when he left the office.

THIRTY-NINE

"Slow your roll girl. Shoot, now you wanna hurry to get to the place after you wanted to go window shopping."

"Kim, you're soo slow," Tina said.

"I'm saying we ain't got to be walking so fast. I got heels on. What if I break sump'n?"

"You ain't gonna break a goddamn thing. Hurry, we're almost there," Tina said. She held Kimberly's hand and dragged her to the entrance of the community center.

"They could've fixed the place up a little better," Kimberly said as she entered.

"You gon' complain all night, bitch? The after party is at Cheaters."

"Shoot, I'm saying, his friends and family could throw sump'n a little better. I'm entitle to..."

"Here comes Miss loud-mouth... Pricilla, hi. How're you doing?" Tina abruptly ended Kimberly's complaints. They turned and sized up Pricilla as she approached.

"Hey girls what's up? You're both looking good, as usual." Pricilla gave both Kim and Tina the once over. "Y'all stay fly. That dancing thing must be paying off, huh?"

"Yep," Tina said.

"And I see that welfare thing still keeping you in Mandy's," Kimberly said. Her eyes were wide, nose flared and, with her hands on her hips, she took a step closer to Pricilla. They were now toe to toe. Pricilla turned, hissed and walked away.

"That's right bitch, keep it moving in your Salvation Army giveaways," Kim shouted.

"Now how you wanna come up in here and start shit and I..."

"I can't stand that bitch. She knows I don't give a fuck. She always dropping hint about the 'dance thing'. Fuck her! Fuck that bitch."

"You know that bitch is soo fucking ghetto. She can't bear to see anybody wid shit better than hers. That' how Ernesto family be coming at you."

"See, you can take that shit, her cousin is your baby daddy. You family. That bitch, don't mean shit to me. And she ain't pay my muthafucking rent. So she better back up before she get smacked up."

"Easy, Kim. Leave that bitch alone. Lets mingle, get some drinks and enjoy the party, ahight."

"What party. These niggas bringing their own brown bags filled with cheap liquor. Damn can't even find a decent drink."

"Come with me. You complain too much. There goes

Mannie and Carlos and them. Let's go over and say hi."

"If you on some political mission, bitch it's too late. The nigga is not here yet. If they didn't like you from way back, they ain't gon' start liking you now. Just chill out one place," Kim said. She gazed across the almost empty room and saw other relatives and friends of Ernesto coming in. Kim heard champagne bottles popping.

"Let's go check out Mannie and his friend Carlos. You know I kind a like his boy Carlos. But he too skinny," Kim said. They slowly made their way.

"It's gonna get crowded," Tina said as she air kissed Mannie and his compadres.

"Hey Tina. Como estas?" Mannie asked.

"Bien, bien. How're you doing Mannie? You remember my girl Kim, right."

"No question. She's still fine. You know the fellas, Carlos and Geo."

"Hi, Carlos." Kim smiled. They both waved at Geo.

"That nigga gonna be real surprise when he get here," Mannie said.

"I thought Nesto was coming with you?" Pricilla asked Tina.

"Oh really?" Tina answered. She looked over to see Kim cuddling up to Carlos. Bitch, she thought. Kimberly nodded then raised the champagne glass to her head. The night felt better and her guards went down. Tina turned around surveyed the place. She saw the balloons, yellow with black letters. Littering the room through the ceiling 'Welcome Home' they all read. White tablecloth covered a table that held a huge diploma shaped cake. There were bottles and a huge white envelope. Tina smiled outward at Ernesto's relatives. The crowd continued to swell. Tina glanced around the room, she saw gums flapping.

Her contemplation was suddenly cut off.

"Everyone shush. He's coming in."

The lights were dimmed and all held their collective breath. A pang of urgency surged through Tina's body and her heart was beating violently against her chest. Ernesto staggered in.

"What the fuck is up? Nobody here but Nesto." His voice was loud in the hushed quiet.

Tina felt her legs go rubbery when she heard him speak.

"This where Geo told me to meet him."

The lights came on and Ernesto De La Rosa's handsome mug rapidly transformed into smiling cheeks. The crowd screamed and descended on him. Ernesto was overcome by the respect shown by his family and friends. He hugged and kissed everyone. In the midst of the excitement, Kimberly appeared from nowhere. Tina found herself crushed by the excited crowd of well-wishers gathered around Nesto. She tried but couldn't get to him before another relative or friend did. She stood and waited for him to approach. She wound up next to Kimberly.

"Where were you?"

"Outside. Why, bitch?"

"Ain't nothing, bitch. I thought you left or sump'n," Tina sniffed at Kimberly. "Saved me any?"

"Yes, slut," Kimberly said. "You know my head-game ain't free, girl," Kimberly said. They laughed then hi-fived. "Your baby daddy is whoa!"

"What you trying to say Kim?"

"That nigga is diesel, brawl-lick. Hmm," Kim smiled.

"He does look good. He got taller, I think." They both admired.

"Is that your stomach growling?" Kimberly asked.

"Yes, let's go get that drink and smoke some o' that 'dro."

The girls walked away as the meet-and-greet love fest continued.

"What's the deal, Tina? I mean, first you were hot to come here. And now that you're here and your baby daddy's running around shaking hands and squeezing ass, you gonna act like you shy, girl," Kim said.

"I don't feel right. You know me, I can't chase no man and that's what that nigga want me to do. He seen me waiting. Yet he made a beeline to his so-called friends. They're more important to him," Kim stared at Tina.

"You wanna go outside and smoke some o' this shit. It's 'dro. It's the bomb, girl."

"Nah, I'm gonna stick around and see what happens." Tina was making eyes at Nesto. This was lost on Kim.

"All right, please yourself. I'm a get my partying on with Carlos," Kim danced away with her dance partner, Lil' Long in tow. A few songs later Tina and Nesto joined them.

"Funny how a little jealousy can bring out our best

moves, huh. Didn't know you had it in ya," Kim said.

"Come on, you know I'm straight up Latina, girl," Tina said.

"You got to show me that move. The one where your leg just kick out like this," Kim said. Her attempt brought her into contact with Ernesto. "Hey, who's that?" Kim asked.

"Hey Kim. What's good, ma?" Ernesto greeted Kim with a hug and a kiss.

"Hi, Nesto."

"Damn Kim, you've been working out? You looking good."

"Yeah, a lil' sump'n, sump'n, you know when I gets a chance to? Not trying to overdo it or nothing?"

"It's working. Got my man Lil' Long sweating."

Kim turned to see the seductive stare of Lil' Long. Ernesto winked and drifted off with Tina.

Ernesto and Tina were alone for the first time all night. He reached over and kissed her full on her lips. She touched his face and giggled like a schoolgirl on her first date.

"It's so good to see you, baby it feels so good to hold you. Those pictures you sent didn't do any justice. You've gotten so, so big," Tina said.

"It's good to see you too, Tina."

"And you're, you know, ah so muscular." Tina took a breath and exhaled. "You got braw-lick and thick." She licked her lips and winked.

Ernesto's cheeks reddened and his smile appeared to be pasted on. Tina had known Ernesto since grade school. His eyes sparkled. Ernesto pulled her close and kissed her full lips hard. She held on floating in his arms allowing Ernesto to take charge. He twirled her round and round, across the floor.

"Wanna come back to my place after this, Nesto?" Tina snuggled next to him, batting her eyes.

Stares followed as Ernesto and Tina made their way through the crowd toward the exit. Ernesto kissed her long and hard in the parking lot. The others joined them and paired off into cars,

Tina pulled him into Mannie's car and shoved an E in her mouth.

"What's that?"

Nesto opened his mouth and she stuffed one his mouth. BMW's peeled out and it wasn't long after that Nesto was over-whelmed by the warm sensation of the drug.

Long after reaching the outskirts of the club, he still felt as if he was floating. Tina watched him sitting in a daze, licked her lips and smile at the possibilites.

By the time Ernesto and Tina walked inside the party was crunked. He spotted Lil' Long slouched in a corner, sniffing coke while rolling a blunt. The feared street warrior stood and received Ernesto with a hug.

"Oh, shit, oh shit. What we got here? A baller?" Ernesto shouted. "How're you feeling, daddy? You looking to get crazy powdered up in here."

"Yeah, yeah, you know a nigga has stay wid da blow and da chronic, dogs."

"Feel you," Ernesto said as he jabbed at Lil' Long's stomach.

"Easy, big fella. You know I took couple of rounds to da ribs, nah mean? I can't too hardly fucking breath as it is." Ernesto sat down and listened to the story of Lil' Long's wounds.

"There's still a contract out on me. Somebody want me and my man dead, you know wha' I'm sayin'?" Lil' Long guzzled.

Sipping champagne and inhaling second hand weed fumes, Nesto knew the words from Lil' Long's mouth held no real meaning but bore a common theme. They were just stories from the streets where there were no winners or losers, just survivors.

"What goes around comes back. Nah mean?" They raised their champagne glass in a toast.

"Salu," Ernesto said and sipped. "You should let Nesto know what he can do to help, homey. You know I'm armed with the Russian connect."

"I got something coming up real soon. I'm gonna call you. You're gonna be surprised by the amount of cheddar you're gonna make in one job," Ernesto said.

"Why are you lookin' out?" Lil' Long asked.

"One hand washes the other," Ernesto said raising his glass. Lil' Long joined him.

Their friendly chatter was interrupted by the deejay's voice. Some club-goers cheered loudly. Both Ernesto and Lil' Long turned as they heard the announcement that Coco was in the house.

"She be puttin' it down right here!" The deejay shouted.

"It's a good muthafuckin' thing I came. That's that rap

bitches I've been dying to see." Lil' Long screamed and walked away. Ernesto stared toward the lit stage where Josephine was singing.

> *I only have one life and I'm gonna live it...*
>
> *Don't know man woman or child gonna tell me how to do it...*

Coco came trudging to the center of the stage. She was hopping and spitting her rhymes.

> *Ain't no nigga around me gon play me and make me a clown...*
>
> *Nah not gonna have never gonna run up on you with fo-fo... real ghetto girls throw your hands up like you dont give a fuck..."*

"This bitch buggin' on stage or what? Nah I ain't having that! Oh no-you a crow-crow. Bitch soo fucking hood, that she's wick-wick-wack." Pricilla stood and shouted.

"Get off the stage bitch and take your man-stealing, no-dancing back-up singer with you!" Pricilla screamed.

She shared hi-fives with Tina and Kim. They relished in having found a common enemy. Tonight, haters were the minority. The single males hooted and hollered for more as Josephine sang demurely and delivered her verse while Coco brazenly trudged onstage. Fans cheered and enjoyed the show.

The combustible combination of Coco's rapping backed by Josephine's singing, mixed in with sizzling dance moves had club-goers hopping out of control. The club was rocking when Pricilla stood up in arms, heckling.

All of a sudden the lights went out and pop... pop... pop...

gunshots blazed, lighting up the stage. Revelers applauded and danced believing the deafening blasts to be a part of the act. Even as security rushed on stage, the club-heads were still partying. The lights came back on and a loud scream was heard.

"Oh my God... oh my God! Someone call a doctor. Pricilla has been shot!"

It was then that club-goers realized this was not a part of the act. They began scrambling everywhere as more gunshots were fired. Members of the club security rushed to where the shots were fired from, but the shooter easily evaded them and escaped using a side door.

By the time the police arrived on scene, the place looked as if a tornado had visited. Minutes later, the whole place was sealed and crawling with investigators.

"Tell me just how did this go down, Miss Coco?" Detective Kowalski demanded grabbing Coco and whisking her from the others in the club.

"Too bad we're gonna have to shut you down from performing Coco. It seems like people gets killed every time you go doing your thing. Is that some kind of coincidence or what?"

"Y'all acting like I'm the one who pulled the trigger. The only thing I was doing was my thing, performing."

"Seems like there are other people out there who doesn't like your performance." The detective said and Coco stared as the paramedics rolled Pricilla's lifeless body out of the club. Nesto and the others somberly brought up the rear.

"How many more people have to die before you cooperate with us? Coco, you know who is responsible for all this killing. Come clean," the detective said shoving a card at Coco.

Deedee and Josephine surrounded Coco as the bodyguards looked on.

FORTY

It was an overcast day. PO Ward's trained eyes searched for any acts suspicious to the ordinary. He sat in the department car with the air conditioner on eating a Gyro. He unraveled the soft-shell and removed the onions. He took another bite, then sipped his cola.

After finishing the food, he swallowed an antacid and burped. He lit a cigarette. He slipped Ray Ban's easily over his eyes.

P.O. Ward had arrived early and drove the entire perimeter, before settling for a spot where, by skillful utilization of his front and rearview mirrors, he could see in all directions. He checked his service weapon and replaced it in the holster. Then he felt for the gun strapped to his ankle.

Every dunk or spectacular lay-up etched that player into the collective conscience of the street-ball hall of fame. The crowd roared after each dramatic play. Fans bet their dollars on players with names like, Shane the dribbling machine and Hot-Sauce and I-B-Right-back.

Street-ballers blessed with immense skills, each player lived up to their own billing. A pass zipped to an open Shane-the-dribbling-machine. The player guarding him left tantalized by his part dance, part dribble. With ballet-like precision, he made another spectacular dunk that sent a buzzing through the crowd.

The game went by but in the back of his mind Ward kept track of the cars coming and going. He saw young guys with Benz and Bentleys. They were festive in baggy, blue jeans and RocaWear gears along with white Tees, throwing down hundred dollar bills in bets of wanton proportions on the outcome of each game.

Ward watched with disdain present on his overworked mug. He checked his cell phone, no calls. That Michael Long must be on colored folk' time, flashed across his mind. He shook the thought by watching the non-stop frenzy of the basketball game as it happened. He waited patiently clicking stills of who-is-who from the high-powered lens of his camera. Before long the applause, shrieks and loud screams that accompanied each sensational play captured his attention.

While Ward became engrossed in the game, Lil' Long crept up alongside of the lawman's car. The crowd was joyous. He got in and immediately pulled out his guns.

"In order for me to remain immortal a-a-all w-we-weak m-m-muthafuckas must di-di-die," Lil' Long said.

Pandemonium broke loose. At that same moment Lil' Long squeezed both triggers.

Loud cheering basketball fans filled the summer night's air and drowned any other sound in the immediate vicinity.

FORTY-ONE

That evening the girls sat in a Mercedes stretch outside the funeral home. They were all dressed in black. A distraught Coco glanced at the crowd drawn to the burial site. Miss Katie would now be laid to rest.

"I don't think that I can bear the sight of someone being put into a hole in the ground," Josephine said and lit a cigarette.

"I'll go with you Coco," Deedee said. Both girls walked to the funeral in progress. Josephine cooled her heels in the car.

"I don't like funerals," Josephine said hugging herself. "Driver, can you turn up the music, please?"

The cigarette appeared to wilt as she nervously sucked on it. She stared out the window as Coco and Deedee disappeared from view.

"I don't know if I can sing, I can't hold my breath," Coco said walking with Deedee. They entered the crowded lobby of the church. She knew she had to participate in the last rites on behalf of Miss Katie.

"You have to try," Deedee said.

There were no dry eyes in the place when Coco's vocals thrilled the crowd and then led the way in a soulful rendition of *Amazing Grace*.

Outside the church, while walking to stretch her legs, Josephine saw a car pulled to a stop. For some unknown reason, her heartbeat increased. From her angle, she couldn't see the driver but immediately recognized the passenger. Josephine raced back to the parked Benz.

"I think I've seen him," she said trying to catch her breath.

"All right young lady, get some air and tell me what you're trying to say."

"I saw him. We gotta warn Coco and Dee. He's here."

"Who's here? Eric?"

"Oh, no I'm talking about him right there," Josephine said pointing to the lurking Lil' Long. The driver cranked the engine and headed in the direction of the burial site.

The grief stricken teens walked hand in hand from the burial site heading back to the waiting Mercedes. The loud honking caught the attention of both girls. Coco and Deedee were caught by surprise. They were unaware that Lil' long had been lurking, but hit the ground when they heard him chanting.

"...all muthafucking bitches must die! Die bitches!"

The Mercedes screeched forward blocking the side-ways aim he had on the girls.

"Oh... fu-fuck y-o-you b-i-bitch-ass!" Lil' Long screamed, rolling out the way of the oncoming car. He recovered, got to his knees and fired his guns at the speeding car.

"Deedee, come on! Get in! Get in quickly!" the body-guard yelled as the car came to a screeching stop next to where Coco and Deedee crouched. The car momentarily blocked Lil' Long's line of fire. The girls jumped in while the guard fired at Lil' Long, distracting him.

"Fuck! These bitches shooting at me!" The street war-rior yelled. He ran and hid behind a headstone. His actions provided enough time for the Mercedes to roar off.

Lil' Long got several shots off before the car went swerving wildly and flew down the road. Bullets went flying by. One tore into the chest of the bodyguard. He slumped as other rounds crashed into his carcass, wide enough to protect the girls.

Lil' Long ran back to his car.

"Follow those bitches!" he furiously screamed. Shocked onlookers quickly jumped to their feet and dialed rapidly on their cell phones.

The Mercedes raced from the cemetery with great haste. A massive explosion distracted motorists, causing cars to skid out of control. The girls watched as traffic conditions became hazardous. The driver held on and steered the car clear of any pile-ups or car wreckages.

"What the hell was that?" Josephine asked.

"I don't know, yo. It sounded like some type of explo-sion. Like a car blew up," Coco said looking around.

"Duck down I think someone is trying to kill us," the driver shouted. Bullets pierced him.

The car came to a rest in the far right lane of the highway. The girls saw another car reverse to align next to theirs. Lil' Long's head came sticking up through the sunroof. With guns drawn, he took aim.

"In order for me to be immortal all y'all weak muthafucking bitches will have to die..." Lil' Long screamed while spraying.

The girls stayed down. Once the gunfire ceased, Josephine peeked out.

She jumped into the driver's seat and pushed his lifeless body aside. Lil' Long squeezed rounds at her.

"Fuck 'em! Fools, they act up and overstep their boundary and now it's my turn. Keep going back, no one gets out alive... No one," Lil' Long shouted.

The driver hesitated when he heard what sounded like sirens above Lil' Long's shouting. He quickly made a move. The car swerved, causing Lil' Long to fall from his perch.

"What da fuck ni-ni-nigga, I had 'em. I had 'em. I could've ki-ki-kill them. Fu-fu-Fuck! Man, fuck you! Wh-what da hell y-y-you doing? Keep backing up, I'm t-t-telling you!"

"It's hard to keep the car straight. Five-oh is gonna be here soon."

"Ya think I care 'bout five-oh? I'm getting' ready to bust. Dogs, dogs, fuck five-oh let me go back and cl-cl-clap at these bi-bi-bitches ma-ma-man."

"I can't go back it's a highway. Someone will crash into us. You got to get at them some other time..."

"Ni-ni-gga, I ain't gonna say it again. G-g-go da fuck back so I can w-e-wet them bi-bi-bitches up." Lil' Long said. He pointed the guns at Geo's head. Geo drove uneasily. The phone rang mercilessly loud. Geo grabbed it as if his life was on the line.

"Dime' lo," Geo said and turned to Lil' Long. "It's Nesto, man. He wants to talk to you, man." He shoved the phone at Lil' Long.

"What up, dogs? You man buggin'. I'm sayin he's soft..."

"I got something big for a couple days from now. It involves millions daddy. Come through and we build on it."

"Ahight." Lil' Long said and hung up the phone. "Yo take me get some food dogs," he requested. The thought of money brought a smile to his frown. It was a large enough sum to defuse Lil' Long.

"You'll get another shot," a still shaky Geo mouthed.

"Yeah, you right. My list just keeps getting' longer," Lil' Long said checking his guns and nodding his head.

They continued riding back peacefully as the sun set on the city.

FORTY-TWO

It seemed like forever that Coco and the girls sat nervously looking around in the car waiting for Uncle E. Josephine turned on the hazard lights. The ticking noise sounded like a bomb about to blow.

"I guess he's back, for real huh?" Deedee said breaking the long silence.

"Hell yes, he's trying to send us back to the essence. He's back for sure, yo," Coco said.

"You think that maybe *he* was the one shooting at us outside the movie theater?" Deedee asked.

"Could be."

"I'm telling you it's like that asshole have nine lives," Deedee said.

"Word up, his ass should definitely be dead already. Look how many people y'all said he done kill," Josephine exclaimed.

"I'm telling you God must have been on our side. The way that nigga pulled up right to the car, yo..."

"My heart almost jumped out my chest when I saw him with them damn two guns ready to shoot. Oh my God. Ah shit that could've been it. No graduation, all that crap my parents put me through..." Josephine coughed as her voice trembled with emotion.

Minutes of silence went by. The girls saw traffic slowing as the police approached from all directions. Deedee was the first to spot the SUV.

"Here comes my uncle." She said as a black Range Rover came to a stop. Eric and a couple of other beefy men jumped out. One of the men with Eric gave the orders. They got in the Range Rover as the two men entered the Mercedes and sped off. Just as the SUV was about to follow they saw the lights flashing and heard the orders from the police.

"Pull over immediately. Turn the engine off and put your hands where I can see them."

Eric Ascot massaged his face with both hands then slammed a fist on the wooden-grain interior.

"Take it easy boss, Mr. Maruichi will fix everything," the driver said as patrol cars sealed the area around them.

FORTY-THREE

Mid afternoon the following day, found Lil' Long along with Ernesto and his cronies, Mannie and Carlos, sitting in a van parked at seventy-second street. They waited across the street from the gleaming York Ave headquarters of Sotheby's, the world famous auction house, listening to the lyrics of Big Pun.

> ...Yeah and you don't stop...
>
> Twenty shot Glock with the cop killer filled up to the top
>
> Yeah and you don't stop...
>
> Joey Crack's the rock and Big Pun keeps the guns cocked...

The group watched and waited for the right vehicle to exit. They knew this particular vehicle would be manned by armed uniformed and plainclothes guards.

"That's fucking crazy, dogs. They got two of the same

type of vans we looking for," Lil' Long observed.

"Tell me what we're going to do?" Ernesto was already on the telephone speaking with someone.

"They want us to split in pairs of two," Ernesto told Lil' Long and the others. "Carlos you stay with this van. We'll meet up later. Mannie come with Nesto."

Ernesto gave the orders. Lil' Long exited the van and got into another rented car driven by Geo. They proceeded behind the armored vehicles.

Before traffic could enter the highway one car wedged between the armored vehicles. There was a stalled construction truck ahead that cut them off from the armored vehicles carrying the loot. The tires of both vehicles were blown out caused by a belt of nails on the roadway. The vehicles pulled over. The drivers exited the armored vehicles to check the tires.

"Let's go! Remember, we're on the clock." Ernesto shouted in Lil' Long's direction.

Cars were slamming into each other while horrified drivers attempted to avoid running into the construction truck. Sand suddenly filled the exit ramp caused from a car slamming into the truck. During the resulting confusion, Lil' Long along with Geo donned their ski masks and raced over to the armored vehicle. They invaded the vehicle with their guns blazing.

When the shooting was over, Lil' Long and Geo grabbed all the marked bags.

"Let's go!" Geo shouted and jumped out running back to the rented car.

"Ahight dogs, I hear you. We good. C'mon we gotta get to the other spot." Lil' Long encouraged after shooting a couple of the guards.

"Si, si, I'm on my way." Geo said and threw the bags inside the car. He readied himself to jump into the driver's seat when Lil' Long shouted.

"In order for me to be immortal all bitch ass mutha-fuckas must die..." Lil' Long said while pumping rounds. Geo leaned closer to hear.

"You crazy. I don't..."

"Tell God I sent you, muthafucka."

"Huh? What you...? Oh shit!" Geo's eyes widened when the heat of the bullets greeted him. He clutched the car door and struggled for a minute. He let go when death gripped his body. It left him on the asphalt bloodied and trembling.

Lil' Long hurriedly left and drove to a secluded spot. He pulled over and checked all the bags. There was a glow from the large amount of diamond rocks that played against the sunlight. Lil' Long packed all the ice in one bag, gathered his belongings then set the car on fire.

Over the next week, Lil' Long laid low under an alias at the Day's Inn. He had food brought to him by ladies of an escort service that he trusted. Every now and then, he would glance at the diamonds until his visions blurred from the glare.

He was sitting in his room watching television when he glimpsed the news of the jewel heist. He smiled when he heard that the diamond that he had taken was worth sixty million dollars. The other item stolen was a vase containing nine Faberge eggs valued over ninety million dollars. The eggs belonged to a Russian billionaire Viktor Vekeselberg. He learned that at the same time they were robbing the trucks, there was also a million dollar jewelry heist. The robbers spoke with thick Russian accents according to witnesses.

At a downtown recording studio, Coco and Eric sat amongst a group listening to music she had recorded. Amidst her vocals, she could hear her voice falter behind the steady drum bass of Hip-Hop. Coco mentally recorded all the people she knew present, including Josephine, Deedee, her friend and fan, Chuck the studio engineer and most importantly, one of music top producers sat next to her and listened intently.

"Rewind that right there, Chuck," Eric said. Coco heard the mistake again, only this time it was very clear.

"We can cover some of those types of errors with ad-libs or we will have to do the whole verse over again until it's right. At different points on the track, I can hear your voice fading. It sounds as if you're waiting for someone else to pick up the slack. You were the only one with the microphone. Your skills are there, you've got to believe in yourself. The listener wants to hear what you have," the producer interjected.

"I hear you, I understand all that you were saying and could hear where my voice is failing, like I ran out of breath." Coco said.

"Don't get it twisted, Coco it's still hot for first time and

I know you'll keep improving. Chuck run a copy of the last song on a CD and give that to Coco," Eric said.

"Thanks..."

"You're doing well. But it's a long way to go. I want you to listen to yourself. Listen close for any other mistakes you feel you made. Then come back in here tomorrow, and turn the place out."

Eric gave Coco a copy of the song on a compact disc.

"What time we start tomorrow, yo?" Coco asked accepting it and as she got ready to leave the room.

FORTY-FOUR

Friday night arrived and brought with it a dreaded feeling for Sophia. Since breaking up with Eric she had engrossed herself totally in her work. She stayed at the office until late hours and sometimes Michael would meet her for a quick dinner, but that would be all her social life entailed. Sophia had no time for the lifestyle and over the past two months, she had not allowed herself to take a break from work. She made herself too busy to respond to Eric's phone calls or e-mails.

Sophia was a trial lawyer already working on six lawsuits. The results were still pending. Her desk had stacks of paperwork, research from the library her assistant had procured. She was currently handling two more cases after just wrapping up three. She really could use a break. When Michael called and promised dinner and Shakespeare in the park, she accepted. He had been calling nonstop and heaved a whole lot of attention her way. He sent her flowers and cute e-mails, despite her reluctance to go out with him. Eventually she broke down and did.

Dinner and the play were great. It was what came after that made Sophia put her guards up. They sat outside an after-hours bar frequented by cops and lawyers. Michael was trying his best to convince her to having a nightcap with him.

"Michael I really should be getting home. I've got so many things to do," Sophia said politely.

"What haven't you done already, Sophia? You've been working so much, I'm surprised the other lawyers don't file a complaint against you."

"My work is appreciated..." Sophia started.

"Why aren't you being appreciated?"

"I am..."

"Then why don't you appreciate yourself?"

"Well I am. I took time off and was out with you when I should be preparing for a trial..." Sophia said and saw that Michael looked dejected.

"See you had to spoil it by mentioning work. Now you know you made a promise and since you broke it then I say we should have this drink together and see where it goes from there."

"I'm agreeing to have only a drink. And I can't be out till the wee hours of the morning..." Sophia said but Michael had cut her talking with his lips pressed to hers. She resisted.

"Okay maybe we shouldn't have anything else to drink." She said but went inside anyway.

Inside the place was crowded and dark. There was an orange neon light that read 'Bar'. There was barely elbowroom anywhere. Sophia stood close behind Michael. He turned around waving two glasses of gin and tonic then handed her one. Michael waved at someone and walked away. She tried to follow him and realized he was going to the toilet. As she waited outside, Sophia saw his friend from the DA's office. Inside he dropped a couple tabs in Michael's outstretched hand.

"Oh these are designed to break down the most timid. And they won't smell when you drop them in her drinks. Soon she will be melting in your arms."

"I only need two, right?"

"That's it dude."

Sophia had finished her drink by the time he returned. Michael dumped her on his friend from the DA's office and set off to get another round.

"You're looking smashing." He offered. Sophia nodded. She hated small talk and really didn't need another drink, but didn't want to embarrass Michael. She looked at her watch at least three times when he returned with more drinks. They drank and Sophia busied herself giving Michael signals. Sophia was ready to call it a night.

A couple of quick yawns later they stood and made their departures. Sophia began to feel woozy the moment she stood. Walking, wobbly, she felt Michael's muscular arm around her.

"What was in those drinks?" She asked on the way to the car.

Maybe it was the alcohol coupled with the fact that she would normally be asleep by this time. Sophia's head rested comfortably on Michael's arms until she felt like he was taking her somewhere unfamiliar.

"Hey, where are we?" Sophia asked sluggishly.

"You're with me Sophie baby," Michael whispered in her ear and Sophia felt an unusual chill crawling down her spine. The hesitation made her suddenly giddy.

"Ha, ha, ha, you called me Sophie baby like you did when we were back in law school together."

"Yeah you'll always be my Sophie baby." Michael said. They entered his apartment with the lights off. He easily scooped her off her feet. Sophia's arms swung freely and her head spun. She held on tighter to Michael. He laid her down on his bed and she watched with drunken amusement as he took his clothes off. Michael stood naked in front of Sophia.

"For the next couple hours or so, I'm going to be your love slave. Tell me anything you want done and it'll be done just the way you want it."

"Michael you're funny."

She tried to laugh but he kissed her and bit her lips. Sophia resisted but she did not push him away. Michael became persistent until she felt his tongue inside her mouth and she wanted to enjoy it, but could smell his cologne. It wasn't a smell she was familiar with. Sophia opened her eyes and watched Michael intensely. She tried to get out of his clutch, he wouldn't let her move.

"You can't leave. You're in no condition to go anywhere." He soothed her with his words. Sophia eyed him defensively. Michael wanted her. His eyes undressed her. He couldn't see her tears as he stripped her naked. Sophia saw his athletic body against the faint light of the room. She wouldn't do a thing, she thought. Not a single thing except lie there and let Michael have his fun.

Michael knelt on the bed next to her staring at Sophia's trembling body. She didn't want to continue, he could tell. Maybe the drug will start working soon; he thought and realized he couldn't stop now. He had seen her recently shaven mound, her shiny nipples sitting on top of perfectly round, soft breasts and Michael did not want to stop. He rubbed Sophia's flat stomach and kneaded her breasts. His heavy dick was so hard it was horizontal by then and laid flat against the lower part of his six-pack. When he stood, Sophia found it difficult keeping her eyes off the total package.

Without saying anything, Michael got closer and Sophia closed her eyes as he kissed her mouth. Sophia's lips were sealed against his determined, probing tongue. He began to lick her nipples in circular motions. He cupped her firm breast in his skilled hands and simultaneously rimmed her nipples with the tip of his tongue. Before long, her soft lips parted and she whispered softly.

"Uh, that feels real good."

Sophia breathed quietly as his tongue action intensified. He nibbled on her nipples, biting gently with his teeth. She moaned softly. Her breasts were wet and supple, they appeared to glow. She wiggled but Michael did not feel Sophia's hands anywhere on his body. He wanted her to touch him but she kept her hands by her side, playing virgin. He rubbed his dick up and down, slipped a condom on then tried to slide it inside her. Sophia resisted.

"No Michael, please don't... please don't..." She choked.

Michael was not discouraged and knelt in front of her

on the bed. He reached under and cupped her buttocks. Sophia reacted by placing her hands over her pubic area. Michael used an impatient tongue to search, while pushing her knees apart. He continued running his tongue up and down her closed thighs until she slipped and opened them slightly. Michael pushed his tongue against her warm shaven skin. His mouth touched her pussy and after running his hand over her mound, her relaxed thighs came apart. He entered her and slammed her hard against the bed. She clung to his powerful forearms as he thrust deep. After awhile he felt her hips rising to match his every stroke. Before long they were completely entangled and he rode on a wave of motion.

Sophia resisted but groaned as Michael touched her in all the right places. She offered little struggle when he swung her legs over his shoulders. He fucked her deep and hard. Sophia felt the pain but could do nothing. She closed her eyes and wished that Eric was here as Michael wildly fucked her. He tossed her and savagely penetrated her ass.

"Ahh, agh... agh oh stop please..." She groaned as Michael rode her fast. Then he pulled out and exploded in her face. "Oh no Michael, please stop. Oh please God, no oh no, oh..." Sophia cried.

She wanted to resist his onslaught, but couldn't muster the energy to fight. Sophia was aware that something had happened and knew she didn't want any part. She was unable to move. She had been drinking alcohol. Nothing was right. Her head pounded and life seemed to drain from her body. Sophia closed her eyes.

Hours passed before she awakened. Sophia felt the person sleeping next to her. She did not feel Eric's hairy chest. She was waking to the smell of another man and did not remember how she got in his bed. Sophia tried to gather her wits and turned and examined the body lying next to her. She didn't hear the door opening. It was too late when she saw the figure.

"Who is there?" Sophia screamed in disbelief.

"Huh, what's the matter?" Michael slowly stirred and yawned.

"In order for me to be immortal all weak ass muthafucka must die..."

"Who is there?" Michael jumped up shouting in fright.

Guns blazed and shells fell in rapid succession. The loud explosion filled the room dulling the shriek of Sophia. He pointed the guns, laughing, enjoying the moment. His mission completed as he fired hitting the target. leaving him in a bloody mess. The barrage lasted for a couple of seconds. Then he walked over and put another shot in his head. Lil' Long smiled. and dropped a matchbook revealing a phone number and a message: 1-800-HIT BODY. WE DON'T STOP.

Sophia tried not to stare but watched his every move.

"I ain't gonna kill you," he said looking at Sophia. She was huddled in a corner and when she saw the lecherous look on his face, she slowly tried to cover her naked body with a sheet. "You that record producer bitch. I got a mesaage for you to give him."

Lil' Long tucked his gun, pulled the sheet off her and grabbed a handfull of Sophia tits. "Dont keep this our secret." He smiled and pushed Sophia back. "Yeah, feel how a real nigga feel."

FORTY-FIVE

The following afternoon, Lil' Long smiled as he watched the news report on television from the bed of a motel. The authorities identified the body as those of assistant district attorney, Michael Thompson there was no mention of Sophia. Ascot's face was flashed as a prime suspect in the killing.

"Nah, nah, don't arrest that muthafucka. Damn, now I gotta go behind bars to kill that muthafucka." Lil' Long hollered at the television, picked up his cell phone and putting the caller on full blast. "Yo, I heard y'all muthafucka looking for me?" He said gruffly.

"Where you been daddy? I thought you were dead. They found your driver dead... and the police have been hanging around here asking all kinds of questions," Ernesto said.

"One thing I wanna know and that is, is it time to collect that cheddar yet, dogs...?"

"Daddy you don't understand, them Russians..."

"Fuck 'em Russian muthafuckas... I see they got your ass

shook. Whatever you say, man. I'll be there at the poolroom at six."

He grabbed the bag with the diamonds and headed out the door. Lil' Long dialed away on his cell phone. "Is this Freddy Maruichi? Yo man I got that and I'm gonna bring it. Have my five hundred Gs' and your jeweler standing by. I don't wanna hear no bullshit outta y'all. I'm on my way." After checking his guns, he hurriedly left. Downstairs he quickly jumped into a waiting taxi.

Coco and Josephine trudged up the stairs of Coco's building. The elevator was broken again. When the girls opened the door to the apartment Rachel Harvey was on her knees, with a man's dick in her mouth.

"What da fuck is this ma? Get da fuck outta here. Get out!" Coco screamed as another man rushed from the bathroom.

The men ran out the door and Coco slammed it shut. The teen locked eyes with her mother. Rachel Harvey scurried off and locked herself inside the bathroom.

In the living room, Coco noticed there were semen markings all over the new furniture. Josephine watched in awe as Coco went to the kitchen, came back with a sponge and began cleaning the furniture.

"That was dumb crazy, Coco," Josephine said. "Parents just do as they wanna like they babies."

Coco's two-way was going off. The message from Deedee read: 'Po-po arrested uncle. I'm at home.'

Coco led Josephine to the kitchen overlooking the streets. They stood their watching the action below for a minute.

"I think I might be pregnant. And it might be Eric's."

"You think or do you know?"

"I'm not sure. It's too early to tell."

"You better ask somebody, Eric was arrested earlier. Dee just sent me a text, yo."

"Get da fuck out! Why they arrested him?"

"For murder," Coco said after looking at her two-way pager.

"Aw man, why shit always got to get fucked up?" Josephine asked wringing her hands.

"Yeah, that's soo hood." Coco said staring at the action on the streets below.

FORTY-SIX

Saturday evening Lil' Long met Nesto at a downtown pool hall. The last time he was here, there was a party like atmosphere. Now the energy was subdued. Nesto sat alone at a table. Lil' Long walked in with his best gangster swagger.

"Hey daddy, hope you brought that with you," Nesto said greeting him.

"You must be loco, dogs. I ain't gonna be walking up in here with all that... I got sump'n better." Lil' Long answered cupping his waist.

"What's that daddy? What could be better?" Nesto asked anxiously.

"I done told you before, dogs. My guns will speak their piece. They will be heard if anyone tries to pull anything."

"Why daddy, we're only trying to get paid our own

money."

"Take me to da man and I'll personally tell him where to find the rocks."

A treacherous screw on Lil' Long's mug conveyed that there was no room for negotiations.

"Done, let's go see da man, daddy," Nesto said.

Later they arrived at the modeling agency and Nesto guided Lil' Long into Karin's office.

"I believe you have something that belongs to a friend of ours," she said. Lil' Long arched his eyebrows and wrinkled his face in anger.

"This ain't Nesto. I ain't shook cuz you Russian, bitch..."

"You weren't saying that when you were getting it in jail from our friends. Well, I just want you to know the same thing can happen on the streets. But why should we have to go there...?"

"Mu-mu-muthafu-fu-fucka, are you thre-thre-threatening me up in here?"

"Oh it's simply not a threat, Mr. Jailbird. It is a promise."

"You talkin' lock up. I ain't doin' no mo'. Never will I ever be taken captive again," Lil' Long yelled. "I'm going out like Kong, taking down buildings and plenty bodies. This da heart of a gangsta! You want da ice? Ya fuckin' diamonds? I got it, bitch. Come get and get this too muthafucka. In order for me to be immortal weak ass muthafuckas and bitches like you must die..." Bullets from twin Desert Eagles went flying at Karin. A short moment of silence followed the spray of bullets, then Lil' Long turned his rage toward Nesto.

"Go ahead pop sump'n. I'm a make this ya funeral too. I'm a keep all da ice and fuck your set," Lil Long screamed.

"No problems from me daddy, but what about...?" Ernesto waved his arm.

"You know what; go ahead cuz i'm feeling generous so I'm a make you live. " Lil' Long said then popped his collar and walked out the door.

Eric Ascot and his attorrney stood in front of a downtown precinct. There were cameras and newspeople all around.

"These irresponsible acts by the detectives of our city should not go unpunished. The officers concerned are constantly violating the rights of the decent people of..."

The lawyer entertained the news hounds gathered. Eric slipped into a Black Benz and was whisked away. His cell phone rang non-stop. Recognizing Sophia's number, he took the call.

"Hello, Sophie. There's no need to be sorry... I've got enough messages from him. I'm just glad you're alright..."

FORTY-SEVEN

It was Monday, a week before graduation. Coco sat in school and glanced around at all the faces. She wanted to scream with relief when she was informed that she was officially the valedictorian. She felt like she had risen from the ashes of a smoldering time. The teachers were showering her with praises. Everywhere she went in the school building, grateful classmates and faculty members greeted her. Coco was in her full bop, when she ran into Josephine and Deedee.

"Silky Black and Show Biz are gonna be using the verses you did in the studio on their new release," Deedee said with a smile.

"You're gonna be a star, girlfriend," Josephine said.

"It's great and all but there's nothing like enjoying it with your true friends. A lot has happened. I mean... Miss Katie was the best person I've ever known in my entire life..."

"Thank God your life ain't over," Josephine joked.

"Word, but I'm saying, we still here. We have to make the best of our lives while we're still here. You know? make things right amongst ourselves and all..."

Coco couldn't wait to get home and tell her mother about the track. She raced upstairs. She reached for her keys.

"Surprise!"

Coco glanced around and smiled when she saw that her apartment was filled with her neighbors. She was showered with hugs and kisses.

"You've got four letters from these colleges. Harvard wants you to come and visit, they offered you an academic scholarship," Rachel Harvey announced.

"Ma, you been snooping in my mail..."

"They right over there next to your cake and the post cards." Rachel Harvey pointed Coco toward the kitchen.

She read the letter from Harvard, Howard, Penn State and Princeton. Coco dreamed of her possibilities.

"Coco that's you rapping on the radio," someone yelled from the living room.

"Turn that up!" another shouted.

Hooting and hollering, her neighbors began partying.

"I must say congrats are in order. Coco, you made the whole community proud. You got the number one smash in the land. Top high school graduate in the country. Highest scores in the SAT over the entire world... smoking on da corners... you such a *fucking* lady, da American dream," Rightchus said.

"Ahight, ahight you said your piece, now git da fuck

outta here," Coco responded.

"Yo Coco, I've been always in your corner down wit' cha. You can't say I ain't been rootin' all the time for your success and this da way you treat me as soon as you start becoming successful. Girl, don't you get above your raisins. Remember where you from..."

FORTY-EIGHT

The following week, Coco and the graduating class of 2003 entered the assembly hall amidst the cheers of parents and family members. Deedee walked proudly with Eric next to her. Sitting in the large audience was a beaming, tear eyed Rachel Harvey. The ceremonies kicked off promptly at nine-thirty.

"Good morning ladies and gentlemen, parents, family members and friends of the graduating class of the year two thousand and three..." the school principal began his speech.

Meanwhile, inside a deli Mannie and a pretty young thing sat next to a large window facing the street. They shared breakfast while awaiting a clinic appointment.

"What time is your appointment?" He asked and watched two motorcyclists parking then walking across the street. They stood as if reading the menu posted outside on the window.

"In fifteen minutes. It's only ten-fifteen," she said glancing at her watch. "You're so impatient Mannie," she added. "Imagine carrying a baby for nine months."

"That's a woman's job, I can't imagine that." Mannie said as he eyed the two figures suspiciously.

His defenses dropped when they removed their helmets. Only two Asian women with long black hair, he thought. Then they opened fire cutting him in half while the girl screamed. Seconds later, they rode off leaving Mannie doubled-over in his chair. The uproar had the other diners running, scattering and screaming.

At the same time the vice principal introduced the Dean of students and the short, balding shifty eyed, bespectacled man made his way to the podium.

"Ladies and Gentlemen, friends and family members, I, too, would like to welcome you to the graduation ceremonies. I have seen some good performances over the past twenty years. What I've been privileged to witness has never happened before, a student achieving a perfect score right across the board. Our Valedictorian did just that. Ladies and gentlemen, I'd like to present, Coco Harvey."

"That's my girl, that's my daughter," Rachel Harvey leapt from her seat and applauded as if her life depended on it.

The audience stood and applauded. Coco made her way to the podium and the chanting began. Josephine and Deedee set it off by clapping in sync to the rhythm of the chant.

"Go Coco, go Coco... Go Coco, go Coco..."

"Yo Coco, kick a rhyme, yo..." an audience member jokingly shouted and everyone laughed.

"She better not," someone said.

The mantra echoing her name continued for five minutes. Coco cleared her throat before beginning her speech.

"Good morning to the graduating class, our families, our friends, and the faculty and staff..."

The applause was deafening and Coco paused before continuing.

"First, I'd like to say thanks. Thanks to all who're graduating, who came to see us graduated and thanks to all the school officials who made all this possible. In the beginning this date seemed so far away and sometimes it became almost unattainable, but thank God for our parents. I guess that's another reason they're here. For those of you who have lost theirs, I want to commend you because as difficult as it is with your parents, I know it is even worse without them. I'd like to thank the people who have supported me, my friends; Josephine and Deedee, you both have been like sisters to me. Miss Katie, God bless you. I love you Madukes."

Coco glanced at her mother's proud face. Mrs. Harvey applauded and the rest of the audience followed suit. She threw her daughter a kiss.

About the same time, Kim awoke and immediately ran to the bathroom. She closed the door and vomited. Carlos was up by the time she came out looking sick. Roshawn ran to her and she picked him up.

"You're ahight, ma," Carlos asked. Kim thought for a while then she answered.

"I hope I'm not pregnant," she said. "I don't need another baby, right this minute."

"We good, ma. Another baby we fine." Carlos said.

"Thanks for your optimism," Kim said sarcastically. "Is my baby okay?" she asked as she walked to where Roshawn lay in the bed.

Last night Kim and Carlos had fell asleep on the sofa. Carlos was completely dressed when Kim and Roshawn walked out. "Mommy loves you baby. Did you sleep well?" Kim asked.

"I love mommy," Roshawn said. Kim laughed as the doorbell rang.

"Must be that crazy ass friend of mine only she'll be up and about..." Kim said and opened the door. There were two Asian women clad in red bikers' suits. "What can I do for y'all?" Kim asked.

"We are here with a message from a friend of Carlos."

"Huh? Carlos? No Carlos lives here." Kim answered.

"Quiene... Who is it?" Carlos asked.

The moment he showed his face, the explosion went off. Kim's eyes widened when she saw the guns. They sprayed bullets through the entire apartment. A fusillade of automatic fire spun Carlos backwards. All the time Kim closed her eyes and hugged Roshawn tightly to her chest. In a matter of seconds the ordeal was over and the killers were gone. Still hugging her son, Kim ran out of the bloody mess that was left in her apartment.

Back in the assembly hall where the graduation ceremonies were in progress, Coco smiled as she continued the valedictorian's speech. Her voice came through clearly and she held the attention of everyone in the audience, especially her mother.

"...we can finally say with pride, we did it. The stress of staying up late night studying, the endless exams, and university applications are all behind us now. There are thousands of memories running through our minds when we reflect on our many high school experiences. I remember losing a dear friend and fellow student, Danielle she was a fun loving person. Despite our experiences good or bad, we have no choice but to grow and move forward in order to realize our dreams..."

The applause was still going when the Dean introduced the graduating class. Immediately after the ceremonies, the girls rushed to pose for photos.

"Here Coco, lemme take one of you and your mom dukes," Josephine said.

"Take another one," someone yelled. Cameras snapped away.

"We've got to go soon because Coco and you have a radio spot and a performance tonight," Deedee reminded.

Flashbulbs popped off when photographers from newspapers and other students recognized him. Coco and Eric took front stage.

Tina and her son was already up when Ernesto awoke at eleven in the morning. He had spent all night hustling in the streets. Nesto yawned and thought of chilling.

"I'm thinking of staying with you and Junior today," he said.

Nesto kissed his son and Tina. He had waited patiently but was having no luck in getting Lil' Long to change his mind. Pretty soon the Russians were gonna make a move, he thought. He was going have to get Lil' Long to turn the diamonds back over to the Russians. No diamonds, no pay day. Nesto sat in the living room watching television. He knew he was running out of time. The doorbell rang.

"Is this Nesto's home?"

"Who is it?"

A Tech nine sprayed. Nesto was left leaking. Tina waited for a couple of seconds, picked up her son and tiptoed over Nesto's bloody carcass.

FORTY-NINE

It was afternoon and the girls were sitting in a booth at the city's hottest radio station. Josephine sipped water and Deedee fidgeted nervously with her cell phone while listening to Coco's first radio interview.

"We'd like to welcome Coco. She's the new sensation from super producer, Eric Ascot. Welcome to the show Coco..." The radio deejay announced.

"Thanks, it's good to be here..." Coco said.

"The phones are already ringing off the hook, the response has been good. I guess callers are anxious to get atcha..." The deejay was in his zone.

"I'm from uptown. I'm ready." Coco and Deedee smiled. Josephine rolled her eyes.

"You're working on a new album with the best producer... you're living your dream, having a top song on the radio. What's been your greatest moment so far, Coco?"

"Without a doubt it's good to work with the best, but graduating from high school I have to say is my greatest moment so far..."

"I'll let the people out there know that you were valedictorian and that's no small thing either. We've got C-O-C-O in the building and I heard her freestyle is nasty, but before she gives us some of that let's take some calls... caller you're on the air..."

"Yeah that's right my girl, Coco... wish all the best. This is your man Naughty from BK... I love the way you do your thing."

"This Tee from da BX and I'd like to holla at my girl C-O-C-O... hoorah! You holding it down for all the hot chicks..."

"Shout out from QB... keep doing ya thing, girl f' 'em 'round da way girls and all the other ghetto bitches..."

"Good-looking out..." Coco shouted while Deedee and Josephine threw high-fives.

"All right, all right we've got time for one more caller before Coco bless us with a freestyle... and do kick a nasty freestyle... Go ahead caller make it short... Caller you're on the air..." the radio jock continued.

"Yeah I just wanna let y'all bitches know that I'm glad you blow cuz now thurrs no place for you to run or hide..." the caller's venom excited the radio jock. He smiled and applauded milking it.

"...That's right folks... the world's filled with haters and you heard it first right here... home of the best of Hip Hop and

R&B... caller state your name..."

"This Lil' Long bitches and I'm coming for ya and I'm gonna kill ya bitch-ass. Yeah, that's right, in order for me to be immortal... all weak ass mutha..."

"Shut your mouth... Oops, I think we've lost that hater..." The radio deejay said smiling and turning to Coco. She opened her parched lips, but nothing came. Josephine hugged herself and was visibly shaken.

Deedee rushed out the studio and was already calling on her cell phone.

"Uncle E... you heard? More security... thank you uncle. I'll let Coco know... see you later."

The radio deejay kept rolling along through the entire fiasco as if it was rehearsed. A hard pulsing drum and bass provided background music.

"That's right you heard it here first, a rapper calling himself Lil' Long calling out Coco... as you know she's in the building... Coco as promised, the microphone's all yours. Let the people hear what you gotta say...I know Lil' Long made you upset but no cursing... Take it away."

Deedee walked back inside the studio and Coco was already in the midst of spitting a fiery gem. Deedee gave her the thumbs up.

> *"A born warrior like Laila...*
>
> *I ain't gonna stand around fearing ya*
>
> *Here's how it's done...*
>
> *My style is second to none...*
>
> *Scars to your face I phantom jab this dagger in*

ya.

put you in your place/

  The pen's mightier than the sword

I might write a check send ya best man to kill ya...

You don't really want it with Coco

  Beat down ya lil' ones it'll be oh no/

  Easy I know I'm on the radio so

Don't get too intense catch me in the hood

I'll end the violence sucka...

  C-O-C-O'll bury ya..."

"You don't have to say no more, ma. What's beef? You heard it right here. Ha, ha, ha." The radio jock laughed.

FIFTY

The execution team known as Calisix had killed Nesto and all his cronies but still no ice had been recovered. They scouted the neighborhood searching for Lil' Long. He was next on the hit list. Rightchus saw the pair, cruising on motorcycles and stopped to flirt a little.

"That's a cool thing to do? Ride and chill in the hood. Maybe I can help y'all beautiful Chinese ladies with best of samplins from the hood. I'm Rightchus and ain't nothing going down without me knowing." He said and limped directly to where they sat.

"Do you know Lil' Long?"

"Not only do I know him, I know why you searching for him. You're looking for the diamonds he sold to Maruichi and..." Rightchus said and one of them pulled out a gun.

"Hold up, easy now, put that cannon away. I ain't tryin' to start no fight with y'all. If I did, I'd come with my kung-fu shit, see you don't know me. I'm a master at this."

"Is there something you're trying to tell us?" One asked.

"I'm saying, is there a reward or not in this for me. I ain't goin' 'gainst Lil' Long with no compensations."

The assassins looked at each other and smiled.

"If you know something, you'll be rewarded for your information."

"Ahight then let's talk pc," Rightchus said. "I did my homework." He added when they gave him a strange look.

The Calisix called for permission to hit the mob. The request was granted and they went after Maruichi.

The family, two brothers and father, sat in the back of the pizza parlor.

"I want those damn cops, Kowalski and Hall dead. I want them dead now." Maruichi yelled. His sons dialed rapidly on their cell phones.

"It's a done deal dad. Those bastards are dead, dad." The words grabbed his father's undivided attention. "I had a wonderful pay off on a huge sum on both their heads. They wont be bothering us anymore, dad." Both sons were too pre-occupied with pleasing their dad. Neither saw when the riders approached the group. With guns drawn, they easily snatched all three and took them home. There they made Maruichi get on the phone and called his lawyer.

"Yeah, you gotta bring that thing here right now." Maruichi ordered. Within minutes, the attorney brought the diamonds and was surprised to see who the buyers were. Once they had procured the loot, the Calisix fired shots in each of the Maruichi's heads killing them. The lawyer was set free.

Rightchus made a call to Hall who was doing paperwork at his desk. He mentioned that something major was going down in the hood. Hall told Kowalski who was ready to jump at the informant's tip.

"We should check into it..." Kowalski said immediately on hearing.

"Give him some time he'll call again," Hall said.

"Let me guess you don't want to play partner? Or the rigors of the job getting to you old man?" Kowalski asked his partner.

"I remember when I was young and dumb like you. I used to jump for everything. I wanted to solve crimes and lock-up criminals." Hall answered.

"I didn't know you could remember that far back." Kowalski shot back.

"Damn right. My partner back then was this old man. He used to try and slow me down. Telling me things like, 'boy, you gotta take it easy'"

"The way you do me?"

"He was one of them good ol' boys and I thought he was being condescending." Hall said looking at the document on his desk.

"There's a point to this story, right?"

"I'm trying to make it if you hold on to your horses. He told me this story about him walking the beat one day when a man ran up to him saying 'arrest me officer, arrest me.' He asked the man 'why should I arrest you?' The man answered 'I was born and surely that's a crime.'"

"All right old man, take your time. I'm going outside to get some fresh air. I'll see you in a minute." Kowalski yawned.

"Give me ten more minutes," Hall said and went back to the paperwork on his desk.

Kowalski walked outside and glimpsed a figure moving quickly away from the back of the gray sedan.

"Hey what're you doing over there? Come here," he yelled.

The man ran and Kowalski gave chase. "Don't make me have to run after you. Halt I said! What the hell!"

Kowalski ran a few more yards after the man. "Halt this is the police!" he screamed and fired ending the pursuit. The man was wounded but still alive. Kowalski moved closer for a better look. "What were you doing to the car back there? Why'd you run?" He asked.

There were no intelligible answers, the victim grunted in pain. Kowalski held the gun on the man.

"You better tell me something..." Kowalski said but the-man had passed out. "Oh no, you're not gonna die, I need information from you. Who sent you?"

Kowalski rifled through his victim's pockets. He gazed at the man's driver's license. Then he saw the matchbook with 1-800-Hit Body WE DONT STOP. He glanced at it, smiled and got on the horn requesting medical assistance.

Detective Hall was finished with the paperwork at his desk. He walked out the precinct looking for his partner. Hall spotted the parked grey sedan and peered through the window. His phone rang just as he opened the door. Hall reached for his cell phone and at the same time turning on the car's ignition.

"Hall, don't get in that car. It's been booby-trapped," Kowalski screamed.

He held his breath as the loud booming sound rocked the surrounding buildings. Kowalski screamed as he pumped several shots into the body of his victim.

Later that night the Calisix met with Rightchus and put a thousand dollars in his hand. He ecstatically tried to kiss the giver.

"Oh shit, oh shit. This is all for me, this all me?"

He jumped jubilantly and yelled until his legs hurt. "Did you get Lil' Long yet?" Rightchus asked nervously. They rode away without saying a word. "I'm a buy me some fly gears, get me a nice girl, oh it's on now, mu'fuckaz."

Not long after they rode away, Lil' Long appeared and saw Rightchus limping on crutches and singing heartily.

"Yeah I got that dough now, see in da stores now, buying all 'em fly gears. That Sean Jean and Akdmiks shit…"

"What da fuck you so happy bout?" Lil' Long asked. "Didn't I tell you not to let me catch your black ass out here on these streets?"

"Yea-yeah, I only came to cop ci-ci-cigarette." Rightchus said. Lil' Long stared at him for a fluttering heartbeat. Rightchus was nervous and trembled his voice shook when he saw Lil' Long's guns. "You already shot me wi-wi-with both yo-yo-your guns…" Rightchus stuttered.

"You trying to mock me, uh nigga? Here hold this then." Lil' Long aimed both guns at Rightchus. "In order for me to be immortal all y'all weak muthafuckas, bitches and snitches must die…" Lil' Long shouted then squeezed the trigger.

"Nooo…"

Rightchus' blood curdling scream filled the air along with the explosion echoed loud into the night's air, then dissipated. Rightchus' fell silent. Lil' Long walked slowly away whispering.

"Snitch-ass nigga, yeah you had that coming. Now I gotta go see them muthafuckin' rappin' ass bitches and that music producer." He said and waved. Seconds later, a taxi pulled up.

"Where to, mister?" The driver asked. Lil' Long took a look and smiled.

"I like you already," he said to the driver. "I'm goin' to see this rap show at club Deep." He said.

"Can do..." she said and drove off. There was a motor-cycle following close behind them.

"Y'all Chinese peeps have y'all hands in everything in da hood, huh?"

"Can do," the driver smiled. Lil' Long relaxed and enjoyed the ride.

FIFTY-ONE

Inside the club there was hollering and hooting as Coco rocked the microphone and the crowd moved to the beat. All through the club the heads bobbed to Coco's masterful flow. She sang and danced, performing magnificently like she never had before.

"Bring that beat down some. This goes out to all my peeps, who may be down and think there's no way they can get up... yeah. I been there, yeah. And I'd like to say thanks to my team, Eric Ascot producer of the year. Uptown's own, Silky Blizack, Show Biz, my girls, Jo and Dee. Yeah... Thanks y'all, I'm still here. RIP, to Miss Katie, my Godmother, I'll always love you. Rip to my girl Bebop, and the one and only Danielle, there'll never be another like her. But life goes on and for that we gotta *give thanks and praises to God..."*

> *When you look inside my life you'll see*
> *Pain and heartaches rolling through me...*

Josephine sang as she bounded on stage. She immediately launched into a crowd pleaser duet with Coco.

> *When you look inside my life you'll see*
>
> *Pain and heartaches rolling through me*
>
> *Can't let that stop me no never not being me...*

The girls sang and Coco busted out her rap.

> *"Yeah, one two it's C-O-C-O...*
>
> *Just clap your hands*
>
> *Everybody act like you know...*
>
> *God gave me the gift to spit this sh...*
>
> *The ability to rise above this sh...*
>
> *You know me sometimes low-key*
>
> *But when I smoke on dro*
>
> *It's like oh no she's loco*
>
> *But I'm straight up being me...Coco..."*

> *"Go Coco, go Coco... Go...Yo, you own this girl..."*

The audience sang along.

> *"Whose house...?" Coco asked.*

"Coco's ..." The crowd roared.

Having pleased the club audience with her verbal skills, Coco dropped the microphone and let her body shake. The uptown flavor of the Hip Hop sound blasted through the speakers. She raised her middle fingers bobbed her head and then bopped off the stage; the chanting of the sweaty crowd rang loud in the air.

Deedee and Eric greeted the girls. They stood offstage watching the featured act. Coco lit a cigarette.

"Your performance was great. Congratulations, Coco," Eric said hugging Coco.

"What about *my* vocals? What am I? Chopped liver?" Josephine joked.

"No, you're not. Jo c'mon girl, you were there too. Coco was in a zone that's all. You both did your thing up there onstage," Eric said.

"I've been crying all day and now most of the night. My eyes can't stay dry. I love you Jo. I'm soo happy for you. Coco you've come along way. Tonight you owned the house." Deedee said and the girls hugged, while Eric smiled.

Outside on the streets, Lil' Long struggled in the back seat of the cab. He wanted to get to the club, but realized that he was not going there. Desert Eagles locked and loaded, he fired at the driver, to no avail. Angrily, Lil' Long ducked as bullets ricocheted off the bulletproof glass that separated driver and passenger. He sat back in the yellow cab.

Further down the road, the driver glanced back to see Lil' Long firing into the door until it was open. She tried to bail out, but the bullets from Lil' Long's guns scorched her flesh. She became distracted and the cab hit an embankment and flew onto the oncoming lane. A motorcycle rolled up to the driver.

"Are you okay?" the motorcyclist asked.

The driver shakily got up and got on the motorcycle.

"We have to kill him." The motorcyclist said. "Igor's word was to bury him alive." They rode off.

Lil' Long crawled with some difficulty, slowly from under the car. Groggily he moved away from the car. He gathered his wits and raced to safety. He hailed a cab.

FIFTY-TWO

Back in the club, the atmosphere was electrically charged with energy fueled by the high-octane performance of Coco and Josephine. Silky Black and the Chop shop Crew got busy and took the excitement to another level with their performance. Club-heads were still going wild as the show drew to a close. The audience was pleased but wanted more.

The group was still in a celebratory mood, Coco and Josephine glad-handed with club goers while giving autographs to fans who sought them. Eric, Silky Black and Show Biz stood talking while Deedee sat cooling her heels, sipping a soda.

"Yo, I'm mad hungry," Josephine said joining Deedee at the table.

"That makes two of us, yo," Coco said pulling out a cigarette and plopping down next to them.

"You both should be exhausted; I know y'all brought crazy energy to that stage tonight." Deedee said and high-fived both girls. They were busy sipping sodas when Eric approached the table.

"All right ladies, looks like you are all tired. It was a great show. I enjoyed every minute of it. Coco before summer ends we've got to finish an album. I think you're ready."

"Thanks, Uncle E."

"Yes I agree." Silky Black and Show Biz gave Coco a hug.

"What about me?" Josephine asked.

"Come on girl, we're a team."

"Me I'm ready to get some shut eye," Deedee said.

"I'm with you on that," Coco said.

"We gonna check out the honeys." Silky Black and Show Biz walked away.

"Let's go," Eric motioned to the bodyguard.

The party was still in effect but the girls were tired. A bodyguard followed closely as all three girls hugged and lumbered behind Eric. Another bodyguard was busy on his cell phone. The group was making their way to the parking garage when suddenly the bodyguard in front stopped.

"What's the matter? You had one too many?" Eric asked. "The Range is over there." Eric pointed.

"I know but our driver ain't responding like he's supposed to."

"He's probably asleep. We've been gone for over two hours..."

A chanting interrupted Eric's words. He turned around to see who it was.

"In order for me to be immortal ..."

The bodyguard in the rear was felled by the blast of two guns.

"All weak muthafuckas and bitch-ass-niggas must die...!"

Again gunshots exploded and the bodyguard up front lay crumpled. A pool of blood formed around his head. It happened so quickly the girls had no time to hit the asphalt. They heard a gruff voice.

"No, no I ain't gon kill y'all yet. Git da fuck up y'all bitches. Yeah nigga it's me muthafuckas. Remember me? I'm the one y'all bust 'em caps in the last time. Yeah, that's right. Luck was on my side..."

"I-I-I wasn't involved, mister. I wasn't even in the city. I was..." Josephine said shuddering.

"Bitch you tryin' to mock me? You better fall back over there with the rest of them 'fore I start with you. Yeah muthafuckas, finally," Lil' Long said prancing around with two guns held high and gloating. He pointed one point blank at Eric's dome and moved in closer.

"Let the girls go and..." Eric quickly jumped in.

"And what bitch ass nigga? You gon pay me off, huh? Don't even think about running to the Range, bitches," Lil' Long said shooting the girls a glance sideways. "I've got bad news for ya, the driver dead and stinking in thurr."

"This between me and you, man... it's got nothing to do with the girls."

Lil' Long appeared amused when Eric spoke. He waved one of his guns side to side. The other, he aimed at the girls.

"Uh huh, it's got urrh-thing to do with the bitches... I didn't know this fine ass black-bitch that me and my man ran up in was your fam, dogs? I know you ain't see the way me and my man dug the bitch back out, so I'm a brake you off a lil' show, an encore you unnerstan. A lil' sump'n, sump'n for making me wait so muthafucking long to kill y'all muthafucking asses already. But first I'm gonna do this..."

Two rounds punctuated Lil' Long's words and Eric fell to the ground.

"Ugh... agh... shit you shot me..."

"Yeah, hold 'em shots and fall back bitch ass. I'm a return you to da essence just like I did that fat nigga, Busta and all 'em cops and wops you sent at me. First thing first: I'm a have some fun and I'm a make sure you stick around to enjoy the show, then I'm a kill your ass." Lil' Long said, grabbed Deedee and pushed her to her knees.

"No don't!" she screamed.

"Chill bitch, you know you want it. I waited a long time for this. Bitch reach up in there and grab hold of my dick and start sucking."

He smiled menacingly and continued.

"Yeah bitch, let your uncle see how well you learned to take my dick. Get it nice and hard bitch," Lil' Long said. Revenge clouded his eyes and his breathing sounded labored.

"I'll pay you whatever you want man, please don't..." Eric begged.

"Shuddafuckup, begging bitch ass nigga! Watch your

niece take some a this real dick." Lil' Long aimed the gun point blank at Eric's dome. "I was in jail dreaming about this moment..."

"Why you wanna play us like that, yo? If you're gonna kill us just get it over with," Coco said.

Lil' Long pushed Deedee away and walked over closer to where Coco stood.

"Oh, I see it's true what they say about you, you got heart, huh bitch?"

"I'm saying yo..."

Lil' Long fired his gun twice and silenced Coco. Josephine tried to jump to her aid but Lil' Long grabbed her.

"Bitch, you move and I'll kill ya fucking ass!" He said.

Josephine's fear left her frozen in tears. Deedee screamed.

"Now you bitch get over here and used all that lungs on my dick. You hear me bitch!" Lil' Long ordered pointing his gun at Deedee. He yanked Deedee roughly by the neck. Josephine's body shook as she cried and watched.

Both Eric and Coco were shot and blood was dripping from them. Eric was still conscious, but Coco was lying uncon-scious. Deedee resisted as Lil' Long grabbed her by the back of her neck and furiously tried to shove his dick in her mouth.

"C'mon now, bitch. Don't front like you don't wanna swallow this."

He slapped her face so hard that Deedee fell back-wards. He stood over her with his guns ready.

"Ahight I see you gon show out cuz ya uncle, huh?

Ahight then fuck it bitch. You leave me no choice... In order for me to be immortal all y'all weak ass muthafuckas and bitches must die..."

There was an explosion.

"Oh shit... uhg..." Lil' Long grunted. He whirled and grabbed his shoulder. One of the guns fell from his grip. Eric immediately tried to reach for it.

"This is the police. Nobody move." Lil' Long looked up, recognizing the face, he smiled.

"What you shoot me for, detective? I was doing y'all po-po a lil' favor and you shoot me?"

"Oh yeah, what favor is that?" The detective asked bending down and ripping the gun from Lil' Long's clutch.

"I know, y'all know that this da king pin right thurr. Eric Ascot, he's got the mob sewn up and he be ordering hits on muthafuckas left and right. Drugs, he running that..." Lil' Long paused to laugh. "Yeah, I'm a snitch on ya... fake-ass music producer." He continued laughing.

"Is that true, Ascot?" The detective asked.

"I don't know what he's talking about. He was trying to murder us. If I was connected, why did he... he tried to rape my niece... again."

The detective's eyes followed Eric's stare to where Coco laid. Deedee joined Josephine and they were both crying over the fallen precocious teen.

"Is that true? Did this piece o' shit try to rape you again?" The detective asked. Deedee nodded. The detective stared at the contortions of pain all over Eric's face.

"Who you gon believe man? Kowalski, we partners," Lil' Long shouted.

"No, we're not."

The detective saw Eric's wide-eyed expression when he unloaded the gun in Lil' Long's body.

"My partner was killed," he said. Lil' Long's body was in death's dance when the detective grabbed Eric's hand and tightened his fingers around the smoking gun. "I want you to know what it feels like to take a life and I want to know the reason my partner was murdered. Do we have a deal?" Kowalski asked.

Eric's answer was barely audible but the detective was satisfied. He was on his horn.

"Gunshots fired, two people hit. Officer needs assistance." Kowalski said.

He shoved the phone back in Eric's pocket after giving the location.

Deedee hurried to Eric and hugged him. He was bleeding but still standing and holding on to the gun Kowalski had given him. Josephine sobbed softly with Coco's head resting on her lap. Blood quietly leaked from the dome of the precocious teen.

To be continued in:

GHETTO GIRLS 4

YOUNG LUV

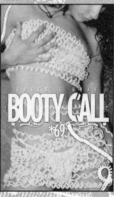

Llanto de la mujer

WOMAN'S
cry

A NOVEL BY
VANESSA MARTIR

Woman's Cry is a Latina look on Hip Hop fiction. It is a Span-glish novella with unexpected twists and turns that will keep the reader enthralled in this urban drama.

Renee Maldonado is a senior at Columbia University and is busy living two opposite lives. Her love for a drug dealer takes her down a dangerous path of trying to hold on to something that's out of her control. She has to turn her life around and realizes that every action brings an unexpected reaction. Renee sees the perilous nature of her decisions and realizes she could gain the world at the cost of losing her soul.

A NOVEL BY
VENESSA MARTIR

A NOVEL BY
JAMES HENDRICKS

THE BLUE CIRCLE

KEISHA SEIGNIOUS

The Blue Circle is a gripping fast paced drama jumping off at the beginning of the Hip Hop era. The explosion of the culture is a visual backdrop. Up in the Bronx where the people are fresh, The Blue Circle was the favorite hangout for b-boys and girls. As the culture grows so does the bond between four friends. Dawn, Keya, Forster, and Cash met at The Blue Circle. Dawn juggles real love with her parents' self centered dreams. Keya is from a decent family, but her life transforms as she struggles with being a single teen parent. Forster and Cash are diehard friends, not even dough could separate them. Starting young in the street game, their pockets grew along with their attitudes. Envy and jealousy threaten these friendships until tragedy occurs. Forster has known Dawn since their teenage days and certainly never considered her a potential wife...until an unexpected heated kiss that brought hope and changes for all. Will they make it down the altar? Or must Forster Pay with his life for Cash's beef?

The Blue Circle is the hot debut novel from a talented writer, Keisha Seignious. Based on a real NYC story, this exciting page-turner examines the scathing aspects of friendship, family interactions and true love.

A NOVEL BY
KEISHA SEGNIOUS

"The Blue Circle is an evocative and shockingly delightful novel that captures you from the very first page!"
— Crystal Lacey Winslow (author of The Criss Cross and Life, Love & Loneliness)

A NOVEL BY
SHARRON DOYLE

it ain't one thing
it's another

A richly textured story of deceit; **If It Ain't One Thing It's Another,** is the most riveting tale of the decade. Every once in a while an author comes along with dazzling talents. In her debut novel, **It Ain't One Thing It's Another**, Sharron Doyle broke us off with this sensational tale of vengeance, thirst and hunger.

Streetwise, Petie is grinding on the road to infamy. His throne is toppled and his rule is coming to an end. He will not be kingpin, but he's bent on taking his family, his mistress, Share', best friend and fellow hustler, Ladell, through their most traumatic experiences. On lockdown, Petie is no snitch and does not cooperate with the justice department. After being released Petie's twisted method of exacting revenge on his enemies will shock and open the eyes of every reader. He comes armed to the nines ready to get rid of those who snitched or betrayed him. Only Share' stands in his way. His enemies soon find out that: **If Ain't One Thing It's Another** is revenge at all cost. Beef never dies, it multiplies.

A NOVEL BY
SHARRON DOYLE

Taking urban erotica to dizzying heights and culminating in an earth-shattering climax, Erick S Gray spins a sexually charged, coming of age tale. The drama in **Booty Call *69** revolves around a promiscuous young woman, Shana, who is so seductive she easily captures any man she glances at. After breaking up with the equally self-indulgent boy-toy, Jakim who is too busy hunting for additional sexual pleasures. Shana finds she's rapidly falling for his best friend, Tyrone and ignores Jakim's attempts at reconciliation. A man will do anything when he loves a woman and will try his best to hold on to what he thinks he needs. But does that mean he has to keep going down the road of mistrust? If you love someone set them free and if the love's meant to be then...

In a hot remix of his Booty Call debut, Erick S Gray shows how unconditional love can be and how grimy trusted friends can get in **Booty Call *69**.

A NOVEL BY
ERICK S GRAY

"Readers, forget what you heard, Booty Call *69 is an orgasmic, spine-tingling, heart stopping tale of erotica."

- Mark Anthony, (Bestselling author of Paper Chaser, Dogism and Ladies Night Out)

It Can Happen In A Minute is a compelling story of love, deception, secrets, lies and making wrong decisions. From the beginning to a very explosive end, S.M. Johnson captivates, titillates and moves readers to tears. Take this journey with Samone who has been labeled the black sheep of her family. Slighted by the ongoing dynamic relationship between her mother and sister, Samone moves from Miami to D.C. But things aren't so good in the hood. She shares life with her father but discovers damaging and grave secrets about him while living in his home. Samone finds herself trapped in a perilous corner where her only escape is to look out for herself. Has she run out of love? And will it be too late to move on? It Can Happen In A Minute is an unforgettable quick ride through heavy drama.

A NOVEL BY
S.M. JOHNSON

"If you're scared of rollercoaster then be very afraid because SM Johnson will hook you and take you on the wildest ride of your life.."

ORDERFORM

NAME _____

COMPANY _____

ADDRESS _____

CITY _____ **STATE** _____ **ZIP** _____

PHONE _____ **FAX** _____

EMAIL _____

TITLES	PRICE	QTY	TOTAL
GHETTO GIRLS (SPECIAL EDITION) / ANTHONY WHYTE	14.95		
GHETTO GIRLS TOO / ANTHONY WHYTE	14.95		
GHETTO GIRLS 3: SOO HOOD / ANTHONY WHYTE	14.95		
THE BLUE CIRCLE / KEISHA SEIGNIOUS	14.95		
BOOTY CALL *69 / ERICK S GRAY	14.95		
IF IT AIN'T ONE THING - IT'S ANOTHER / SHARRON DOYLE	14.95		
IT CAN HAPPEN IN A MINUTE / S.M. JOHNSON	14.95		
	SUBTOTAL		
	SHIPPING		
	8.625% TAX		
	TOTAL		

AUGUSTUS
PUBLISHING

MAKE ALL CHECKS PAYABLE TO:
AUGUSTUS PUBLISHING / 33 INDIAN ROAD NY, NY 10034 / SUITE 3K
SHIPPING CHARGES
GROUND ONE BOOK $4.95 / EACH ADDITIONAL BOOK $1.00

AugustusPublishing.com
info@augustuspublishing.com